DEVOTED
TO AN
Outlaw

A NOVEL BY

DAK

Royalty Publishing House is now accepting manuscripts from aspiring or experienced urban romance authors!

WHAT MAY PLACE YOU ABOVE THE REST:

Heroes who are the ultimate book bae: strong-willed, maybe a little rough around the edges but willing to risk it all for the woman he loves.

Heroines who are the ultimate match: the girl next door type, not perfect - has her faults but is still a decent person. One who is willing to risk it all for the man she loves.

The rest is up to you! Just be creative, think out of the box, keep it sexy and intriguing!

If you'd like to join the Royal family, send us the first 15K words (60 pages) of your completed manuscript to submissions@royaltypublishing-house.com

SYNOPSIS

Biz is the founder of Dead Silence, the most lethal company for murder for hire. When he's paid for one of his very own assassin's murder, he knows that it can be a great thing or horrible. When it comes to pleasure and business, is Biz capable of separating the two without getting his own hands dirty?

Rashad aka Havoc is a real nigga who goes after anyone who hurts his family. When his best friend Khalil is killed, everyone is in for feeling his wrath. Anyone associated with his death is in for a rude awakening, even if his twin sister is one of them. To him loyalty is everything, but it seems like he is the only person in his world who believes that.

When Bonnie falls for the enemy, she's stuck between a rock and a hard place having to choose between her twin brother Havoc or her man Biz. Although Biz had betrayed her trust, he still holds the little bit of love that she has left in her heart. When the two men she loves the most are at each other's throats, which side is she supposed to pick?

PROLOGUE

*B*iz sat in his office as he held the name of one of his best assassins. He had started his organization Dead Silence when he was in his early 20s. He had recruited a dozen people who he took in and Biz called them his very own twelve disciples. He had taught, trained, and molded them into the perfect killers. The job of murder for hire never got old; there was always hate in the world. Someone always wanted someone dead and was willing to pay the price to get it done. Dead Silence handled business for the top-notch people in the game. He had handled hits for politicians, kingpins, billionaires, you name it. No one wanted to get their hands dirty but always wanted to play dirty. If the price was right, the job could definitely get done. To the world, there was no such person named Biz under his description, and that also applied to his twelve workers. Twenty years in the game and business was still booming.

Biz rubbed his beard in frustration, knowing what he had to do. He had just received a wire transfer in his offshore account of five million dollars, a name, and photo of one of his very own assassins, Khalil. He knew it was a dangerous game he was playing. Biz hadn't gotten his hands dirty in over ten years, but the person who put out the hit on Khalil wanted Biz to personally handle this. Biz didn't know whose feathers Khalil had ruffled, and he didn't bother to ask. The less people thought he knew, he figured was best. All he needed was a name, a picture, and his money and from there, Dead Silence handled it. It took him and his team from about five hours to five weeks to get the job done depending on the difficulty. For the right price they'd put anyone to sleep, his own assassins weren't excluded. Biz knew what had to be done and was ready to just do it like Nike.

He dialed Khalil's number off one of the many burner phones he had and waited on an answer. "Yo K, got a name and a place, meet me there alone. I'll text you the address," Biz said into the phone and then hung up. He looked over at the picture of Khalil that was sent one last time before shaking his head and lighting it on fire. This was a ritual for every picture he got. He memorized the name, did his research, and let his disciples handle the rest. He texted the address to Khalil then headed out the door. He was ready to make this quick and easy. He had pretty much raised Khalil and the other eleven assassins. From day one, he let it be known to each of them that no matter how close they got Biz would never take it personal. Whether they knew it or not, Biz meant it very much.

* * *

"DROP ME OFF AT THIS ADDY," Khalil said to Havoc as the text of the address came through from Biz. "It's 23251 Elmer Pike Dr," he read off to his best friend Rashad, better known as Havoc.

"It's a one-man hit?" Havoc asked skeptically as he made a wild U-turn and headed to the address.

"Man, I guess. He told me come alone so I'm assuming it is," Khalil said strapping up. To Khalil, a two-man hit could always be carried out by one person. He knew he'd be straight. He was always clean, and his aim was steady so he didn't have a worry in his mind. After about twenty minutes, they were there. "Aight, imma hit you up later," Khalil said hopping out the whip.

Havoc was still on edge for some reason. He never questioned Biz though because he knew he meant well. Biz almost never sent out one-man hits and Havoc knew the water had run dry for Biz so he was definitely not going on a hit. He drove around the back, parking in a cornfield, hiding as Biz pulled up. Biz got out his car and looked around as he always did making sure to be aware of his surroundings. This had become a habit for him.

Biz entered from the back door and as soon as he was in, Havoc crept around the cornfield and looked into the crack of the door. It seemed as if time sped up to a million minutes per second, as Biz swiftly pulled out his silenced CZ-P10 and emptied his rounds into Khalil without even giving him a chance to speak. Havoc knew right at this moment there wasn't anything he could do. Biz had the senses of a dog and the reflexes of a cat. There was no way that he could sneak up behind Biz and try to kill him. At this moment, Havoc realized he had to come up with a master plan. Biz had to go and he vowed from that day forth, he was going to avenge Khalil's death no matter the consequences.

1

SWEET REVENGE

"It's breaking my heart to watch you run around, 'cause I know that you're living a lie."

— JUSTIN TIMBERLAKE

*B*onnie sat reclined on her couch as Biz did his thing in between her legs using his big, fat, juicy tongue. She had fucked with him for the past nine months just to get close enough to him to kill him. The longer she was around him, the harder she fell. She had learned so much about her boss in the past few months, he had shown her a side of him that no one knew existed. She was plotting her revenge for her man Khalil who died at the hands of Biz. She knew that any minute she'd have to reach between the couch cushions and put two bullets in his head. But before she did that, she wanted to get her nut off. Biz literally had the best dick she'd ever experienced, and his tongue game was even better. There was no denying the head he gave as his tongue flicked on her clit and his fingers penetrated in and out her ass. "Oh shit Biz, right there daddy!" she screamed as she put her fingers through his locks and pulled his hair. The harder she pulled the faster his tongue flicked across her clit. As soon as she was about to nut, the front door came crashing open which startled the both of them, causing them both to pull their 9mm out the couch cushions and to aim at the door.

The two felt one another's betrayal as Bonnie put her piece down and snatched Biz's then began scrapping around the floor for her shirt and skirt. Her brother Havoc burned a hole in her back while she did, without taking his aim off Biz. "I told you put a hole in this nigga's head, but you don't fucking listen! Had I not made my grand fucking entrance, this nigga would've wasted you B!"

Bonnie looked at Biz as he held a smirk on his face. "I peeped game a while ago, just was waiting on the perfect moment to put two holes in your head," Biz said before chuckling. "You really had a real nigga that was down for you and only you, but you was too busy being blinded by the revenge of Khalil's death. That's the damn problem! Motherfuckers don't know how to separate business from pleasure. Khalil's death was all business! They don't call me Biz for no motherfucking reason!!" Bonnie stood right beside her brother also pointing both guns at Biz. "I made y'all! Khalil, Bonnie, and Rashad were no one! Y'all welcome!" Biz added.

The more he talked, the more upset Havoc got. "You ain't make shit nigga! You the grimiest, most disloyal nigga I ever met! Khalil was riding for you till the wheels fell off and you fucked it all up." Havoc let two shots go, one in his chest and one in his face. The sound of the shots caused Bonnie to jump and her heart to drop. She had killed many people with no remorse, and watched mothers die along with their newborn babies and never felt like this. A lone tear slipped out her eye and as she went to wipe it, Havoc put his pistol to her head. "You going soft over this nigga?!" he asked as he pushed the barrel of his gun harder onto her head.

"Nigga stop fuckin' trippin' and call the damn maids and have them come clean up my damn house," Bonnie responded, brushing it off. Havoc stared at her dead in her eyes for another five seconds looking for a sign of weakness in his twin sister so he could put her to sleep right beside the nigga that turned her soft. But Bonnie refused to give Havoc a reason to kill her. She knew he'd do it. He had absolutely no love for Biz. Biz was the reason they were as cold as they were. The reason Khalil was gone. He put the gun down before turning to walk out the door.

Before walking out behind him, Bonnie ran over to Biz's body and felt a faint pulse. She quickly dug in his pocket grabbing his phone, as she looked at the door hoping that Havoc didn't come back inside for her. She knew if she got caught, she'd definitely be dead. She dialed Biz's personal doctor friend that he had on speed dial. "Come get Biz at 4547 Westwood Avenue. Get here ASAP! Cleaning crew is on their way," she quickly said into the phone and hung up, stuffing the phone back into his pocket. She pressed her lips against his and whispered in his ear, "I love you Biz."

As she got up and turned around, she saw Havoc going for his gun again. She didn't know how much he saw but she knew it couldn't have been much because she was still alive. "Relax, you trigger happy ass nigga. I was making sure he didn't have a pulse," she said as she began walking towards him. Havoc kept his hand on his pistol while watching his twin walk out the door. All he wanted was for Biz to be dead, since Biz was the cause of his right-hand man's death. As Bonnie walked out, Havoc followed behind her. "You called the maids already, right?" Bonnie asked as she took a seat in Havoc's all-black Rolls Royce Ghost.

"Yea, we don't have any targeted names yet and you can't come back to your crib until tomorrow, so where you gonna stay?"

"Drop me off at Harper's crib. I'll stay there till we get a name," Bonnie said while reclining her chair and closing her eyes. Her heart was heavy at this moment and all she was hoping was that Biz was going to make it. She didn't want to show Havoc any signs of care, so she stayed quiet the whole ride.

BONNIE SAT on Harper's couch twiddling with her fingers with Biz still on her mind, hoping and praying that he was alive. She looked over at Harper who was indulged in the Nature channel, then at the table where Harper's keys were. Harper was the only normal part of Bonnie's life. The two were complete opposites. Bonnie was an assassin that resembled Naomi Campbell, except with fuller lips and hips that Shakira sang about, standing at six feet tall, the color of Godiva chocolate with 4A hair that touched the middle of her back and natural booty like Amber Rose. Harper, on the other hand, was a neurosurgeon, four feet tall and could pass for Erika Sawajiri. The two were literally like night and day but had been best

7

friends for over a decade. Harper knew all about what Bonnie and Havoc did for a living. She thought it was interesting. She would always wait for Bonnie to tell her stories about her missions. The two balanced one another's lives. What one lacked, the other didn't.

Bonnie glanced at the car keys on the table then back at Harper who was oblivious to the fact that Bonnie's mind was somewhere else. "Harp, can I use your car to go grab something from my house?" she asked, impatiently waiting on an answer.

"Sure, be careful 'cause I'm pretty sure the maids ain't done cleaning up your place."

Bonnie snatched the car keys up from the table and headed out the door. She had told Harper the details of the events that occurred in her house, leaving out the part where she called someone to get Biz. She hopped in Harper's Porsche and sped over to her house doing 50 mph, turning a twenty-minute drive into ten minutes. With the car barely in park, she jumped out and rushed over to one of the workers. "Y'all finished cleaning?" she asked the obvious.

"Yes, um did you guys get rid of the body yourselves? Because it wasn't here when we got here." That was Music to Bonnie's ears. She could finally breath again.

"Yes, I took care of it," she replied while walking away. As she got in the car, she put her head against the steering wheel taking another deep breath and thanking God.

2

ROCKABYE BABY

"Spring turned into summer, and summer faded into fall. Turned out he was a missing person nobody missed at all."

— DIXIE CHICKS

"We been seeing each other for a while now, when you gon' let me show you a good time?" Mark Andrews, who was a key witness to a mafia murder, said to Bonnie. Bonnie had been able to get close enough to him to have him leave his security of the night. It was crazy how sloppy a nigga moved for pussy. A pretty face was enough for motherfuckers to put their lives on the line even when they knew there was a bounty on their heads. She didn't know if Mark was stupid, or if he just didn't see how serious all this shit was. But to her, it didn't matter. She was about to make a bag off of him and he didn't know it.

"We've been having a good time; don't you think so?" Bonnie teased, knowing exactly what Mark meant buy a "good time." He loved playing these games with her. They'd been seeing each other for about three weeks now and like Bonnie thought, tonight was THE night, that she'd seal his fate. She had him smitten and this shit was just too easy to her.

Mark leaned into her ear and began to whisper. "Having your thick, juicy, black pussy against my tongue would make our night ten times better," he said as his soft lips brushed across her ear. To any other female, this sounded like a day in heaven. But to Bonnie, she had heard all this before and if it wasn't from the right nigga, she'd stay dry as sandpaper. Mark was far from her type; he stood at a solid five feet, skin was white as clouds, and he had a receding hairline worse than Lebron's. All Bonnie could think as he continued to speak and brag about how good his sex game was, *this pussy will ruin your life white boy*. But she didn't wear her thoughts on her sleeve. She made him feel like he was saying all the right things when in reality her trigger finger was itching to take care of him.

"How about we go to the motel down the street and I put you to the test and see what you working with little daddy," she said, running game on him the same way he thought he did to her. He tossed his drink back and put his arm around Bonnie's waist and the two left the bar. A smirk adorned Bonnie's face as all the other white women who thought Mark was the shit began to send jealous stares her way. They had all heard of the pending case and the fact that he was alive and still breathing made women want to get next to him. If the mob couldn't touch him they figured nobody could. Bonnie was smirking because she felt like she had one up on these white bitches. First, because she knew that behind their jealous stares nothing but racist thoughts were in their mind, and secondly, because she knew the real shit. By the end of the night, Mark would be a memory of the past.

Bonnie drove her rental because of course her date didn't have a whip, but that was beside the point. She never got into a target's car. Biz had trained them to never let their target have any trace of them. Bonnie drove to the motel and as soon as Mark hopped out to get a room, she turned and grabbed her purse from the backseat. Her princess was in her back with her crown on and all Bonnie had to do was pull the trigger to conclude her mission. Bonnie sat in the car fixing her makeup and her pink wig that she wore on her head. Her hairstylist Kym had definitely slayed her unit and there was no denying it. As she looked through the windshield, she saw Mark coming out with the room key in his hand. She was ready to do away with him already. It was only three in the afternoon and she had other things to do than to babysit a snitch.

As soon as they got into the room, Bonnie excused herself and went into the bathroom. "Hurry up in there babygirl. I can't wait to put my face between your legs," he said.

"I'm about to blow ya mind baby," Bonnie said as she rolled her eyes and pulled out her princess, then walked out the bathroom. Before Mark could even speak, he dropped both glasses of wine and like clockwork, Bonnie let off two rounds straight into his head. His body went limp almost instantly, and she walked over to him and checked him for a pulse. After confirming her job was done, she grabbed a wet wipe out her purse and wiped off the bathroom door handles. She chuckled to herself because in her mind, she had warned him.

She walked out the motel room and once she got into the rental, she texted Havoc a thumbs up so the maids could come finish off her job cleaning up the mess she left behind. Bonnie then snatched off her wig letting her neatly done flat twist show.

* * *

HAVOC WATCHED like a hawk as his target kissed his pregnant wife goodbye for the day. He had no idea that today was the day, the day that he would be saying his last goodbyes. Havoc had been nice enough not to slay his entire family, but he didn't get that sympathy. Havoc was playing the grim reaper and he was here to collect. He watched as he jumped in his car driving to his office. Today was the day that he was due for a raise. A raise that he would never get. Havoc drove behind the car close enough to keep him in his sights but far enough to not be made. As his target pulled into the parking garage Havoc did the same. He parked two cars down from him and grabbed his taser from the center console. He could've killed him right here right now, but that would've been too easy of a death for him. He wanted him to suffer a little. He hopped out his car and walked over to the 5'9 framed man. Before he could figure out what was going on, Havoc's taser met with his neck long enough for him to pass out.

* * *

11

HAVOC HOPPED out his 2016 Aston Martin DB9 and walked onto Khalil's gravesite. He, Bonnie and Khalil had invested in their own cemetery where they could lay bodies down easily. The three of them buried any and everything at this site. They had handpicked out the very exact spot where they'd be buried at. They knew in this line of work they were gonna be gone one day and they had no clue what day exactly it would be, but they were at peace just knowing where exactly they'd be buried. He did the sign of the cross as he stepped in front of Khalil's tombstone, his friend was finally able to be at rest. "B and I got that nigga for you bro. Shit ain't the same, watch over us my nigga," he said as he stared at the words on the tombstone which read *Khalil Alexander Mack, brother and Lover, February 14, 1986 – December 22, 2016 Fly High.* In a few months, it was about to be a complete year that he was gone.

Havoc had gotten rid of the person who killed his best friend, but now it was time to find out who put the hit out. After staring blankly at the tombstone for about five more minutes, he did the cross symbol one last time before walking away. He hopped back in the whip and blasted his music up to drown out the kicking sound in his trunk. He drove to the other end of the cemetery and stopped at the hole he'd previously gotten dug up. This was a special hole and he was throwing his own funeral service today. He popped the trunk and Manny, Biz's right-hand man, was in there. Havoc knew he'd taken care of Biz already, but he still felt like he had to cut all loose ends and Manny had to get it too. He was sealing his fate simply because of being personally associated with Biz. He lifted Manny out the trunk and threw him onto the ground. Manny didn't bother begging for his life because he already knew whether he begged or not, he was gonna end up in this hole. He knew Havoc, Khalil and the rest of the disciples just as well as Biz did. Manny knew Havoc would come after Biz and himself one day. He just didn't think today would be his day. If he had known, he would've kissed his wife a little longer, and hugged her a little tighter. One day it would be Havoc's day, and he just hated the fact that he wouldn't be around for it. The angry look on Havoc's face caused him to smirk. He knew that Khalil's death still had him bitter. The two were like Paul and Cody Walker. They had treated one another like brothers for so long that Manny thought that maybe they believed they actually were. The way that Havoc was carrying on about Khalil's death, he knew that if it was vice versa Khalil would be going about shit the exact same way.

"You not even gonna beg for your life even a little, and act like a little bitch and all that other shit pussy niggas do before death?" Havoc spat with nothing but venom in his voice.

Manny looked Havoc dead in the eye and replied, "I ain't never been a pussy nigga since you met me. Only nigga who was gonna beg for they life after getting in this game was Khalil; let's just thank God my nigga Biz didn't give him a chance." Manny chuckled at the thought, knowing that he was taunting Havoc. Although his arms were tied together and so were his legs, he managed to hop into the hole that was made specifically for him. He laid in the hole and closed his eyes as Havoc picked up the shovel and began covering him in dirt. As he felt the dirt cover him, images of his pregnant wife were all he could see. He just wished that he was able to kiss her a little longer before he left the house if he knew it would be his last kiss. He knew in his heart that he would always be with her; he had given her a miniature him and she would be good. She would mourn him but she would be fine and that alone made his death go by a little easier.

3

BLOOD IS THICKER THAN WATER

"If I die today or tomorrow, I guess I'm outta luck."

— MASTER P

*H*arper sat of the ledge of the tub holding Bonnie's hair up as she bent over the toilet puking her guts out. "Damn bitch, you got a virus?" Harper asked. This was the second time today that Bonnie was vomiting.

"Nah, I think I have food poisoning. On the date I think I ate bad seafood from that bourgeoisie ass restaurant Lé Cuisine," Bonnie said right before vomiting again. "I'm giving them motherfuckers one star and writing the most terrible review ever," Bonnie added as she inhaled and exhaled quickly.

"Bitch, clearly this was a date gone wrong. Your damn date was probably trying to kill your ass before you got him," Harper joked.

"Haha, very funny. I always get them first though!" Bonnie replied, grinning at the thought of a target's attempt to kill her but her being two steps ahead at all times. It was almost like a sick game to her. She stood up and began brushing her teeth.

"B, imma head home so I can fix dinner before Chris and CJ get home," Harper said as she gathered her purse and coat. "Stay hydrated boo," she added while walking out the door. Bonnie gave her a head nod as she walked behind her to lock it. Before she could completely close the door, Havoc stuck his foot in it.

"What you been up to twin?" he asked, making his way into the house and walking straight into her kitchen. Bonnie locked the door and walked over to the sink to rinse her mouth. While doing so, Havoc opened up her refrigerator taking out her carton of orange juice. Instead of grabbing a glass, he put the carton to his lips and began gulping it down. Bonnie dried her mouth and began to walk over to Havoc to curse him out for the bad habit he had but before she could even make it to him, she could feel vomit in the back of her throat.

She rushed to the bathroom but was too late. The floor was covered in vomit and she held her own hair up as she continued to dry heave. She had thrown everything up already and there was nothing more for her to vomit. Bonnie's vomiting instantly rose red flags to Havoc. "Ain't this about a bitch! You pregnant with this nigga baby?!" Havoc asked while walking up to his twin sister and yanking her hair back like she was a random hoe in the street.

"Havoc, get the fuck off me nigga and stop acting like you my damn daddy," Bonnie replied as she punched him twice in the face causing his lip to bust. This only infuriated him. With his hand still in her hair almost ripping it from her scalp, he threw her across the room and into a wall causing her to get a gash above her eye. As the blood trickled down her face, the first thing she thought was death. She didn't care that he was her brother. She'd always vowed to herself to never let a man put his hands on her. She jumped up to her feet and the two of them stood in a fighting stance. They fought all the time and it was always over the same reasons. Havoc thought she was his wife or kid instead of his twin sister. Anytime they'd get into it, Khalil would step in before it went too far, but now that Khalil was gone they were fighting like cats and dogs. The two knew how crazy a fight between them could get, and that was why any other time they would both get a few hits in to rile one another up then drop it. But this was that one time that shit went too far, and the only way they wouldn't end up killing each other was if God himself came down and separated them.

Bonnie's eyes resembled a lion who was hunting his prey. Havoc had seen that look in her eye two other times in his life. When Bonnie killed their dad and when she killed a mother who had tortured and killed her child. That look meant one thing, that someone was about to die. Like clockwork, Bonnie swiftly grabbed a Ruger LC9 out the bottom cabinet of her bathroom sink, and Havoc pulled out his Glock 9mm from the concealed holster that he wore. The two stood head to head with direct aim at one another and blood going down their faces. Without flinching, Bonnie pulled the trigger letting a round go off and into her twin and moving so his bullet wouldn't hit her. As the bullet hit him in the shoulder, he too pulled the trigger and a bullet grazed Bonnie on the side of her shoulder. "Ahh, you fucking cunt!" Bonnie yelled as she held her shoulder.

"Bitch! YOU SHOT ME," Havoc yelled back as he sat up putting pressure on his shoulder. He knew if Bonnie wanted to kill him, she would have done so. Her aim was A1 and if she wanted to get him in the heart, she would have. The two sat there looking at one another, pissed. Bonnie really wanted to end him, but he was literally her other half. They had always been side by side and there was no way she'd end that, at least not because of his dumbass making false accusations. "Come on and kill me," Havoc taunted. He knew saying that to her was like playing Russian roulette, but he loved the adrenaline rush.

"Shut the fuck up you stupid fuck," Bonnie responded while getting back on her feet and walking away from him, and back into the kitchen to grab her phone. She dialed Harper's number and put the phone on speaker as she looked at her wound.

"Who are you calling?" Havoc asked as he stepped back into the kitchen while putting pressure on his bloody wound.

"Nigga stay still! Tracking your fucking blood all over my fucking house," Bonnie fussed. Just as Harper answered her phone, she could hear her bestfriend fussing at her brother.

"Hello."

"Harp, 911," Bonnie said. She knew Harper would be on her way as fast as she could. The two had made "911" their code long before Bonnie told her what she was into. It was like a cry for help that could mean anything from men problems, to life or death. Whatever the situation, they were always there for one another.

Bonnie and Havoc sat in the kitchen giving one another the evil eye. Both wanted to end one another but didn't know how life would be without the other. "How you gon' do that to my nigga, Khalil?! How the fuck you get pregnant by the enemy?!" Havoc yelled, making himself even more angry.

"Shut the fuck up! Just because I fucking throw up, that does not mean that I am fucking pregnant! If you throw the fuck up, does that make your bitch ass pregnant?!" Bonnie yelled furiously. She was so through with Havoc trying to be her dad. She knew she wasn't pregnant and Havoc's dumbass assumption was what had his ass sitting there shot.

"So, take a pregnancy test," he suggested. Something in his body had him feeling like his twin sister was pregnant and he wasn't going to let it go until he knew for sure.

"Nigga fuck you! Suck my dick," Bonnie responded, offended. She didn't care if Havoc didn't believe her. She didn't need to prove shit to him. Havoc clenched his jaw because he knew Bonnie was trying to get under his skin even more. Before he could give her a piece of his mind, Harper's special knock was at the door. Bonnie took one last look of disgust and annoyance at her brother before walking to the door and answering. "Harp, can you stitch this bitch ass nigga up, while I get myself ready to handle some business?" she asked rhetorically while walking towards her bathroom.

"What the fuck happened in here?" Harper responded, baffled. She followed the trail of blood into the kitchen and laid eyes on a weak Havoc sitting on the ground. She quickly rushed over to him grabbing a towel out the hospital bag she brought with her. She put pressure on the wound which Havoc had done stopping most of the bleeding. "Hold this right there," she said, getting up washing her hands and putting gloves on. She rushed to the bathroom where Bonnie stood in the mirror stitching up the gash above her eye. "Pass me the alcohol," she said while observing the stitches Bonnie had done. *I taught her well*, Harper thought to herself. Bonnie passed her the alcohol and Harper dashed back into the kitchen. "Squeeze something 'cause this boutta hurt like hell," Harper warned Havoc.

"Ling Ling, just do your thing. I ain't no punk," he replied ignorantly, causing Harper to roll her eyes. Havoc's ego was bigger than Kanye's, and Harper knew that this was gonna be painful, but she said nothing more. Seeing him in pain would be something she would get a rise out of since he thought he was Mr. Tough Guy. She removed the towel from the wound and poured half the bottle of alcohol onto it. Havoc clenched down on his teeth and balled his fist so tight, his nails dig into his hand. Harper knew he wanted to scream like a little bitch but the kind of man he was, he refused to show any sign of weakness.

She pulled a tweezer out her bag and fished for the bullet. Once she finally got the bullet out, she poured the rest of the remaining alcohol onto him. The sight of him in pain made her smirk. "You over there grinning while a nigga all fucked up. I don't see what the fuck is funny," Havoc said. But Harper paid him no mind. She pulled out some bandage wrap that she kept in her bag. Bonnie walked out the bathroom with a bucket filled with bleach, Lysol, ammonia and a gas mask on.

"Get the hell off my damn floor so I can clean up your nasty ass blood," Bonnie said. Havoc and Harper instantly began coughing. Harper already knew that if she didn't hurry the hell up, the toxic gas could kill them both. Bonnie poured the deadly combination on the floor and began scrubbing. Harper stopped what she was doing to open up the windows in the kitchen to let the gas out. But that still wasn't enough. Her and Havoc were coughing their lungs out. She grabbed two paper face masks out her bag and passed one to Havoc. She quickly continued to wrap his wound, meanwhile her eyes were watering.

"Bonnie, I swear you one crazy bitch. Scratch that! Y'all some retarded ass damn twins," Harper said. "Havoc, we gon' have to take this outside 'cause my damn eyes are burning," she added. The gas smell went straight through her paper mask, her eyes were tearing, and her nose was running like a snot-nosed little kid. Bonnie didn't care one bit. She was on a warpath right now and she didn't care who she hurt.

4

LIFE OR DEATH

"Damn! We was supposed to rule the world baby. We was unstoppable, the shit can't be over."

— B.I.G

$\mathcal{H}$avoc and Bonnie sat side by side at the white tie event. The two looked stunning, like the perfect couple. Bonnie donned a white Roland Mouret pencil skirt that hugged her hips, showing her curves, and a Fashion Nova halter top. Her Bantu knot out fell loosely over her shoulders. The 50k gold necklace and earring set was blinding. Her makeup was done so neatly and dramatically she resembled a Nubian goddess. Havoc had all the ladies drooling at the mouth with his fresh cut and diamond-studded earrings. He kept it simple with a crisp, white Roberto Cavalli suit and some gators on his feet. While Bonnie walked around mingling, Havoc kept his eyes on the prize.

"Not only did you cheat on me with that bitch and get her pregnant, but you had the audacity to invite her to OUR white tie event! The fucking nerve of you," Kimberly scolded to her husband in his ear. She was furious with his carelessness for her and her feelings.

"Come on Kim, not today. This isn't the time nor place. Drink some wine, have some fun. Mariah is over there minding her own business and here you come with all the bitter bullshit."

"Mayor Reed, can I please take your lovely wife off your hands for a minute?" Havoc asked charmingly, with two drinks in his hand.

"Please do," Reed responded. He walked away from Kimberly and Havoc heading straight for Mariah. Mayor Reed didn't have a type of woman by the looks of his wife and his mistress. His wife Kimberly was a white woman with no booty, blonde hair in a short bob and a set of perky Ds. Whereas his mistress Mariah was some kind of mix of nationalities with a set of hips that were hypnotizing, long, jet-black hair and eyes that were to die for. Kimberly just watched him in disgust. She didn't know what she had done so wrong in life to deserve a man so arrogant like Reed.

"I want that bitch wiped off this fucking earth ASAP," Kimberly stated as the steam blew through her ears. Kimberly and Dead Silence organization went way back. She had once been a disciple but was able to get out and change her life and identity. It was rare of Biz to let a disciple go. To him, there was only one way to leave Dead Silence and that was in a grave. But Kimberly was one of a kind, she was dangerous. The way she assassinated people it was like a ghost came in a room and stole a soul. At least that was how Biz described it. But that life was behind her now. Every day she dreamed of putting that bitch Mariah to sleep. Instead of getting her own hands dirty, she decided, why not make a few phone calls. She knew for the right amount of money, Havoc and Bonnie would clean shit up.

"Be cool soul snatcher, you know how the game goes. It's gone get done," Havoc said, calling her by her old nickname. He and Kimberly went way back. They tested the waters with one another and both decided it was best to leave that situation alone. They were so crazy about one another they had almost killed each other numerous amounts of times. Kimberly watched her husband in disgust as he drooled over Mariah. As she stared with envy, Havoc just shook his head. He had always vowed that he would never fall in love. He had seen love do crazy shit to people and he wasn't here for it. It was better Kimberly than him in this position. He watched as Bonnie poured half a glass of thallium into a glass of wine. The amount she put would put Mariah to bed in five minutes tops. She grabbed the glass and walked over to the mayor and his mistress.

"Evening Reed, may I please have a word with your beautiful wife?" Bonnie spoke sweetly, charming the hell out of both of them. Neither one of them corrected Bonnie and she knew that they wouldn't. He just flashed a million-dollar smile and kissed Mariah on the cheek, embarrassing his wife before walking away. Bonnie and Mariah both watched as he walked right back to his wife.

"I want her to rot somewhere, so I don't have to share my man anymore," Mariah whispered while pouting like a kid who didn't wanna share toys.

"In due time, let's toast to it," Bonnie suggested while passing Mariah the glass of wine. "To becoming Mrs. Reed," Bonnie added. The sound of those words coming out of someone else's mouth who wasn't her or Reed flattered her. She absentmindedly downed the drink and within two minutes, she was sweating profusely.

Havoc and Kimberly both looked over at Bonnie as she put her hand on Mariah's back and led her to the bathroom. Kimberly knew exactly what was going on and she had dreamt of this day for years. She wanted to watch the woman who had ruined her marriage die a slow, painful death. She walked to the bathroom shortly after Bonnie and Mariah had walked inside. She saw Mariah standing over the sink with blood coming out of her nose and mouth. She smirked and grabbed a paper towel, tossing it at Mariah. "Clean yourself up, bitch," she joked.

Mariah smirked as well as she saw Havoc standing behind Kim with a .380 and a silencer. "Checkmate, bitch," were her last words as she fell back into the wall knowing this was her fate. Before Kimberly could even figure out what Mariah was talking about, Havoc let off two shots to her dome. Bonnie stood right beside her brother as he let one last shot go into Mariah's head for assurance purpose. "If this is what love does to you, I'm good love, enjoy," Bonnie said as she walked out the bathroom and straight out the ballroom with her brother right behind her.

5

MIA

"God isn't dead, he's just missing in action."

— PHIL OCHS

*I*t had been a month since the lick on the mayor's wife and mistress. Havoc had been running around handling other business affairs he had going on. And Bonnie was just doing what every woman loved to do with her free time, shop. For some reason, Biz was heavily on her mind. All the hope that she had that maybe he had survived went out the window, and that ate her up alive. He had shown her the way a man should treat a lady. He made her feel like a school girl who was head over heels for her bad boy. The way she felt in his presence she had never felt before, not even with Khalil. She was a gangster bitch; she didn't know if the feeling was normal, or how to shake the feeling off. She had killed two women in love with the same man and knew that she'd kill a nigga before she let him play those games with her. To her, every nigga played the same games. They entertained a pretty face and fat ass until they got tired of looking at it. Then it was on to the next one. She knew before she let a nigga walk out her life, she'd bury him.

Khalil had been her one exception. No bitch could get near him and it took him years to pull Bonnie. The two met when they were 12 and were inseparable since. Bonnie let Khalil know from jump, she wasn't the one to play with. After witnessing her murder game, Khalil knew she was serious. She didn't give chances. All he had was one time to fuck up and she would be done with him. Khalil took that one chance and never fucked up. Bonnie was his queen. He worshipped everything about her. To him, there was no woman like the one he got. He felt like he was Jay Z and she was Beyoncé and somewhere along the way, he'd gotten lucky. Just the sight of Bonnie made his dick stand up, and Bonnie knew very well how to satisfy her man. The thought of Khalil made her heart flutter. The love that they shared was a love so special, and she knew it. She thought about her man daily, and no, she wasn't hurting. They had both known the lifestyle they lived and that their survival wasn't guaranteed. She knew she wouldn't mourn forever. Three days was the most she mourned for, then it was back to regular programming. Khalil was gone but Bonnie was alive. The most she could do was avenge his death, which she had done. But somehow, guilt consumed her. She had fallen for the enemy. She had lost her first great love, Khalil, and never thought she'd love again. But she was wrong. Biz had captured her heart and there was nothing she could do about it. That was the thing she hated about love; you couldn't control who you loved. The heart had a mind of its own. Bonnie felt lucky to have experienced two loves in one lifetime. Khalil had taken a piece of her with him, but the part of her that was still alive wanted to just live her best spontaneous life.

Bonnie shook the thought of Biz and Khalil from her mind and walked up to the register to pay for her things. She pulled her phone out to pay with Apple pay and realized that Harper had shot her a text. *"Come over, need to talk to you. Important,"* the text read. After paying for her items, Bonnie placed her phone back into her purse. She had a hair appointment and was almost late. She grabbed her bags and walked out the boutique.

As she began walking towards the rental she was using, she felt a presence behind her. She slowly slid her hand in her purse reaching for her pocketknife then she felt the barrel of a gun on her back. "Shit!" she said under her breath. She had no idea what was going on and who was after her, but what she did know was whoever it was, wanted her alive because if they didn't, she would be dead already. "HELP!" she yelled, trying to get the attention of bystanders. But the person behind her used the gun and pistol whipped her with it causing her to fall out.

* * *

Havoc sat in driver side of his matte black, 2016 Maserati Ghibli as his old hoe Vee did that trick that involved his dick in the back of her throat. Vee was something to do when there was nothing to do. There was nothing in the world she wouldn't do for Havoc. His cleanliness and his swag were what made her pussy wet from the first time she saw him. His presence commanded power. She didn't give two fucks about what he did for a living, hell she didn't give a damn about his lifestyle and whether he had a wife and kids at him. She felt lucky just having him in her presence. She didn't care about the money he gave her after sucking and fucking him. All she cared about was getting some good dick from him. Then he could go his way and she could go hers. Havoc pulled on her hair and thrusted his hips fucking her face, feeling his dick hit the back of her throat. Vee could feel the veins popping out from his dick and she knew that meant at any moment, he was gonna cum. She removed her mouth off his shaft and onto his balls while jerking him with one hand and using her other hand to play with her clit.

Havoc began counting down in his head the seconds before he was about to nut, bracing himself for the euphoric feeling while also telling himself mentally not to make a sound like he always did. It was one of those things that his ego was too big for. He didn't want to give any women the satisfaction of hearing him moan like a bitch. He nutted and Vee rubbed his cum all over her face while removing her mouth from his ball sack and onto his dick licking up all his kids and sucking him until there was no more cum left. "Damn Vee, keep doing a nigga like that and imma keep coming back," Havoc said while pulling his drawers and pants up. He meant what he said, but Vee knew the only reason he'd come back was because her sex was immaculate. She knew Havoc wasn't getting tied down to anyone, and she was okay with that. She just felt like the minute he changed his mind on that, she would be first in line. Havoc felt like he had hit the jackpot meeting Vee. She let him go as he pleased and that's what he wanted. No strings attached. As much as he enjoyed whatever they were, she enjoyed it as well. She was out doing her and wasn't the relationship type neither. Like two matching puzzle pieces, together they fit. Havoc pulled out ten hundred-dollar bills and put them in her Tory Burch purse. Vee paid him no mind as she slipped her strapless dress on and fixed her hair in the mirror.

"Next time, imma get us a room 'cause that dick is something that I need to feel in me," Vee spoke while applying her nude color lipstick.

"I'll pullup when you do," Havoc responded while starting up his car. Vee gladly grabbed her purse and hopped out and strutted to her car. Havoc stared at that ass she was packing and shook his head before peeling away.

Once he got on the freeway, he dialed his sister's phone number and she still wasn't answering. He had been calling her for three days and he couldn't get through to her. He had called Harper to see if she'd spoken to her, and it was no luck. He had even stopped by her house a few times and there was no sign that she had been home. Disappearing wasn't Bonnie's thing. In fact, to Havoc it was hard as hell to get Bonnie out of his face. Never the one to worry, suspicion took over him. In their line of work anything was possible. In his gut something was wrong, but he couldn't tell what. He and Bonnie had protocol set in place that if they didn't communicate in over a week then something had gone wrong. A week wasn't up so Havoc could do nothing except play by their rules to truly know if something was wrong with his twin sister. He had to keep the money coming in though and that's what his mind was on. Getting to a bag.

6

CAPTIVE

"I could lure you in, I'm so clever with it. There's really nowhere to run so you could just forget it. I set a trap and ooh, look how I caught you in it."

— CHRIS BROWN

*I*t had been a week since Bonnie was snatched off the streets and she was still locked in a dark garage, with her hands and feet tied together. Although there was no way out, every day she looked for a way to escape. Whoever kidnapped her was taking their time. They wanted her to feel crazy and violated. They weren't through with her yet because every day she was fed some kind of food. After attempting to bite the person who fed her, she was starved for an entire day. She knew that whoever had ordered her kidnapping was trying to punish her like a kid. But she didn't care. Every day she'd spit, bite, kick or even try to headbutt whoever it was trying to take care of her. She wasn't going out without a fight and everyone knew this at that point. She wasn't herself. For the first time, she actually felt crazy. In the line of work she was in, anyone could be her captor. She always knew in the back of her mind she could have the same fate she delivered daily, but that was a day she always tried to avoid.

That was why she was always on her Ps and Qs, but the day she was taken off the streets she was off by a little bit and that wasn't normal for her. Bonnie could be everything in the world but off her game was never one of the things she was. She had no idea why she was in the predicament she was in, but she was determined to find out. As she looked around the garage to see if she could find something to help be set free, like she did every day, she heard the locks on the door twisting and turning. She already had in it her mind that whoever it was wouldn't be leaving alive. She had made up her mind that at this point, everyone was gonna get it. If she was about to be killed, she was gonna go out with a bang and put up a damn good fight. She had been chill and nice, playing the game her captor wanted to play, and now it was time to do things her way.

She mustered up all the energy she could get as the door opened. The light from the outside began blinding her and all that she could see was a silhouette. She sat still as the person began to walk towards her. She anticipated his every move. At this point, she knew he had been the man she wanted to see. She could tell by the way he walked. His powerful stride screamed "Boss." She waited till he got closer to her and knew that at this point, it was do or die. When he got close enough for her to see his face, just when she was about to kill him with a nail she'd pulled out the seat she was sitting in, she stopped dead in her tracks like a deer caught in headlights. A lone tear slipped her eye. "Biz?" she whispered, barely making a sound. Only saying it loud enough for the two of them to hear.

"That's right, I'm back from the dead baby," he said while kneeling to face her at eye level. Bonnie couldn't believe her eyes. She hadn't seen or heard from him in months and assumed the worst. She thought about him every day and whether she knew it or not, or cared to admit it, he made her heart skip a beat. She was in awe and happiness took over her as her heart began to beat a mile a minute. He cut her hands loose and she reached her hand up to touch his face. Letting it roam until it touched the bullet wound that her brother had put into him. She winced at the feel of it, only imagining the pain he went through. She wanted to make sure that this was real. *Is he really here?* she asked herself. She had been sitting in the dark long enough to even be hallucinating. She touched and rubbed his skin as she remembered how smooth it was and her hands went down touching his chest, and the packs that she loved to let her hand roam so freely on were there. She let her hand rest on his heart, and it was no coincidence that both of their hearts beat in sync.

Biz allowed her to touch him because he knew this would be the last time she would ever touch him. She had deceived him once and he would not give her a chance to do it twice. She should have been dead days ago, but he just had to see her one last time and feel her, breathe her air. Bonnie had been his weakness before, and he knew that if he kept her around, she'd truly finish what she had started out to do. She did something to him that he couldn't explain. She had penetrated a wall no one had ever been able to tear down. Whether he chose to admit it or not, Bonnie had melted the ice around his heart, and he had trusted her. But her deceit was what reminded him why he didn't trust a soul.

As tears trickled down her face, the strings she had attached on his heart pulled. He would never reveal that Bonnie had been the forbidden fruit that he couldn't stay away from. Bonnie knew this was it. Biz was the past that had come back to haunt her. Knowing her life was on a ticking time clock, she took in everything about Biz that she could. His Creed cologne made her pussy throb. The scar from his face made her want to kiss all over him. The smell of his cologne made her want to lick all over him. Everything she wanted to do, she knew she'd never get a chance to do. But Bonnie was desperate, and desperate times called for desperate measures. She closed her eyes the minute she saw Biz put his hand behind his back. She let the tears fall freely as she heard him pull the hammer back on the gun that he had just pulled out his waistband. He put his pistol to her head and said his final words to her. "Goodbye Bonnie."

With her mouth just inches from his, she pulled in a little closer feeling the fullness and softness of his lips. As if she felt the anticipation of his finger slowly curving around the trigger, she took those seconds to say her last words. "I'm pregnant."

Her words were barely above a whisper but Biz heard her clear as day, and the revelation caused him to pull back as memories tugged at his heart and flooded his mind.

7

THE PAST

8 YEARS EARLIER

"You realize that our mistrust of the future makes it hard to give up the past."

— CHUCK PALAHNIUK

"I'm pregnant," Cynthia repeated while looking at the stone-cold face Biz had on. Biz tried not to show any emotions as the words left her mouth. Cynthia was a stripper that Biz enjoyed dipping his dick into from time to time. The two had a strict sex only rule. They both agreed to fuck only one another but there was no attachment. Biz felt absolutely nothing for her, and Cynthia had mutual feelings. HIV rate was too high and neither of them wanted to catch the monster. They allowed each other to explore the bodies of one another. After sex between the two, there was no pillow talking. They strictly released a nut and kept it pushing. Sex was always in a hotel. They had both agreed to keeping their personal life private. Biz was almost sure that sexually, Cynthia was the female version of him. Unlike these other women, her vagina wasn't the direct line to her heart. Sex was sex, which was amazing, but that was exactly all that it was. Amazing sex. Cynthia, a full flesh Haitian woman with curly hair standing at five foot two inches, couldn't believe it. She had been told a few years before meeting Biz that she couldn't bear children. The shock she felt was the shock of her life. With or without Biz, she was keeping her baby. She wanted to give Biz the option of being there for their child. He was still in shock. The thought of having kids had never crossed his mind before. And now that there was a bun in the oven, he was no coward. It was time to step up and be a man. He knew the life he led was risky, but he was still willing to protect the family that he was unknowingly building.

Biz rubbed his head in frustration. Not frustrated at the news, but frustrated over the fact that now he had to change the way he moved. He knew word could never get out about a child of his, and he was gonna make sure of it. Without a word, he walked out the hotel room leaving Cynthia sitting there alone. She knew that was his final answer. Although he hadn't spoken a word, he had just let her know a baby couldn't be brought into his world. She knew whether he wanted to be an active parent or not, she was having her a baby. This baby was like a miracle for her and she refused to let anyone steal her pride and joy. Like a bad bitch, she stood up and walked out the hotel room. Now, she wasn't only thinking for herself but for her baby as well.

The very next day, Biz pulled up outside of Cynthia's door. Although he had never been inside, he made sure to know where she rested her head way before they even began fucking around. Biz was a thorough man and anyone he let get close to him, he knew all there was to know. It was his killer instinct. He'd rather have been able to get to someone before he let them be able to get to him, and Cynthia was no different. He hopped out his black Cadillac and smoothly walked over to Cynthia's door. She hadn't answered his calls, figuring that all that he would try to do was convince her to get an abortion, but it was non-debatable. He gave three light knocks on the door and waited for an answer.

Cynthia walked over to the door and opening it and her brows raised in surprise. "What do you want?"

Biz looked down in her hand and saw a book titled *How to really be a mother?* "Got an extra book for me?" he asked while flashing a grin that Cynthia had never seen before. Although the two had never felt a thing for one another, they felt something for what they created. Biz pulled keys out of his pocket and passed them to her.

"What's this?" she asked nervously.

"Get dressed and let's go," he commanded, and Cynthia did just as she was told. The two sat in his vehicle as he drove two-and-a-half-hours. Finally, they had pulled up to a gate where Biz punched a code in. There were security guards everywhere that Biz had paid for to ensure Cynthia and his unborn child's safety. Biz pulled up to the circular driveway and parked before turning to a sleeping Cynthia. "Cyn, wake up." He nudged her before hopping out the car.

The minute she opened her eyes, her jaw fell to the floor. "What's this?" she asked again, as if it wasn't obvious. But the twenty-acre mansion was too much to take in.

"It's for you and the baby," he said while walking towards the house. Cynthia was right on his heel. Nothing went unnoticed from the fountain outside to the playground in the backyard. Unbeknownst to Cynthia, the minute Biz left the hotel room, he had gone to purchase this home for his new family. Cynthia was now his family whether he knew it or not and although they weren't in love, they had one thing in common, and that was their baby.

As the months went by, Biz spared no expense on their baby girl. She was due any day now, but nothing stopped him from handling his business. A baby meant more responsibility and more responsibility meant more money. He saw Cynthia only when it was needed. He knew they'd be the perfect parents because there was no emotional attachment to one another. It was simply as if he was her sperm donor and she was his surrogate. He was a man and was making sure that the mother of his child needed nothing. Anything Cynthia thought the baby would need was delivered to the house. By her third trimester, her baby had more things than she would ever use.

Cynthia was nine months pregnant and ready to meet her baby girl. She waddled to the kitchen for her midnight snack because tonight she was craving nachos and cheese. The minute she opened her refrigerator, water began rushing down her legs. Not the one to panic, she took deep breaths as her contractions began. She attempted to walk up the bedroom stairs to grab her phone and call Biz, but the pain she felt was too much to bear. She sat on the kitchen floor as the pain worsened. There was nothing she could do but lay down and scream in pain. She heard the locks to the door unlocking and couldn't be happier. Biz walked into the kitchen and knew that he had to act fast. He had gone to medical school for a few years, but never in his years of life had he experienced anything like this. Before he could prep himself, he could see the baby's head peeking from her vagina and knew that he had no time to think. He was no doctor, but he was sure it was time for her to push. He grabbed a kitchen towel and filled a cup with scorching hot water before grabbing the kitchen scissors and putting them into the water sterilizing them. He sat on the floor facing her vagina as she screamed in agony. Biz couldn't lie, this was some superwoman shit and it made his dick hurt to watch.

"Push Cyn," he coached as the baby's head began to slide out. He continued to coach her and after about four pushes, their baby girl Isabella Marie was screaming at the top of her lungs. Biz used the scissors to cut her umbilical cord. Childbirth made him respect women in a different way. He saluted any women who could give birth to a kid. After letting Cyn see the baby, he helped her up and got her and the baby cleaned up. He placed a call to one of the only people he trusted with his life, Doc.

Within an hour, Doc was at the house examining Cynthia and Isabella. He waited as they both slept peacefully. Unbeknownst to Cynthia, while Doc examined Isabella, he swabbed her mouth. Biz trusted no one's word and before he could break his walls down for a baby, he had to make sure she was his. He let Doc do his magic and leave.

Within an hour, Doc was calling Biz. "Negative," was all he said, and Biz hung up. His eyes got cold and he had to leave the house. He had already had in his mind and trained his heart on the fact that he had a kid and now that he didn't, his heart was colder than ever. He walked out the house and never looked back, leaving Cyn with everything that he had purchased. A day later, Biz received another call from Doc notifying him that his sperm count was low and his chances of getting a woman pregnant were slim to none. The news to Biz weirdly made him happy. Now he never had to adjust his lifestyle again. Or so he thought.

8

THE PRESENT

"Love is not something you feel, it is something you do."

— DAVID WILKERSON

*B*iz so badly wanted to end Bonnie right where she was, but her revelation was like music to his ears. *That's impossible,* he thought to himself while taking his finger off the trigger. *If this bitch is pregnant, it ain't mine.*

As if she could read his mind, she spoke up again. "I haven't let anyone go in me raw Biz. You were my exception." All he could think was there was no way. Bonnie had opened a wound that he had closed years ago. Biz knew his chances of having children were slim to none but deep down inside of him, he wanted a child to pass his legacy down to. If Bonnie was telling the truth, this would be his chance.

In Biz's twenty years in the game, he had never hesitated to kill. But here with Bonnie was different. She made him feel different, and he had no idea if it was a good or bad thing. He withdrew his gun from her head and Bonnie silently thanked God as he walked out the room without saying a word. She had never been so close to death. She felt like she had bought herself some time. She didn't know what was going through Biz's head, but she just hoped and prayed like hell for the first time that she was pregnant. She knew that if she wasn't then it would be the end of her, but it was a gamble she was willing to take. Bonnie knew something was up with her body and she was almost sure it was pregnancy, although she would never admit it to anyone, especially not Havoc. She had gone soft and the corner of the room reeked of vomit and feces. Her body felt like it wasn't hers and mentally, she knew the only thing it could be was pregnancy.

As a million thoughts ran through her mind, she finally felt the urge to vomit again. She pushed herself onto the ground and held the vomit in as she slid on the floor to the corner of the room and released her stomach of the water she had been given. She hadn't eaten in three days and she had no strength in her. She just hoped Biz would let her go, that whatever chemistry she thought they had would be enough for him to just turn a blind eye to what she did. But somewhere in her heart, she knew if she wasn't pregnant that he would dispose of her like she never existed.

While she dry heaved in the corner, the garage door opened once more and the lights came on. She had no clue about what day of the week it was or the time of the day. She felt like a prisoner in solitary confinement. The lights made her feel the same way prisoners felt knowing that it was time to go back to their original cell. She squinted her eyes trying to adjust to the light. When she came to, she saw Biz and Doc walking up to her. Biz's face was unfazed while the stench in the room made Doc's face turn sour.

Doc tried holding his breath as he walked over to Bonnie to draw her blood. He really just wanted to pass her a cup to urinate in, but he wanted to be absolutely sure. Doc and Biz went way back. They had met when they were thirteen and off the back vowed loyalty to one another. They had the kind of friendship that even if they didn't speak for years at a time, when one needed the other, they'd come running. Their loyalty ran deep. As Doc drew her blood, Biz stared at Bonnie who was just nodding off. She was drained and seeing her in this state made him feel like he needed to care for her. He wanted to hate her but no matter how his mind felt, his heart felt the complete opposite. This was a first and he didn't really know how to deal with that fact.

When Doc finished, Biz let out a deep breath. He didn't even realize that he was holding his breath. As Doc walked away, Bonnie stared at Biz and he felt as if she was staring into his soul. Her eyes said every word that her mouth couldn't. "I'm sorry," she said in a faint whisper before falling out. Biz felt himself panic, something he never did.

"Doc!! COME HERE NOW!" he raised his voice. He knelt over to Bonnie and touched her neck to see if he felt a pulse. Her pulse was faint, but it was there. His mind was racing because he couldn't figure out why he cared so much if she did die. The hate that he felt for her after being betrayed always seemed to melt away when he and she got in the same vicinity. The chemistry between the two of them was so strong that neither one of them would stand a chance.

Doc rushed into the room passing Biz gloves and a needle. "Let's start an IV, she's dehydrated," he said as he prepped the saline bag. Although Biz had done some years in the medical field, Doc had been his teacher before that. Doc had showed him the ropes which had even inspired Biz to go to school. There had been a time when Doc was in medical school and Biz was his test dummy, and they drew blood from one another.

As they stabilized her, Doc put his hand on Biz's back and led him out the garage. "What are you going to do if she's really pregnant?"

"I need a DNA test before I make a final decision," Biz responded. Doc nodded his head. He had been friends with Biz for over two decades and he could see the difference in Biz and how he was with Bonnie.

"You feeling the broad like that?" he asked knowingly while passing him a swab.

Biz took his hand and ran it through his beard as he shook his head trying to figure that out for himself. "It's complicated, and I believe that the only thing that can come from the two of us is complications."

Doc nodded his head one last time before entering the garage and gathering up his things. The last time Biz had gotten wrapped up with a woman, her deceit changed him, and not for the better. Doc didn't want to see history repeat itself because he knew that Biz would be on a rampage. "Aight baby, imma hit the lab and hit you as soon as I get these results," Doc said while opening the baggie for Biz to drop the swab into and heading back towards the door. Biz nodded his head while trying to continue his thought process of what was next. "And bro, please get her cleaned up," Doc added before completely walking out.

* * *

AFTER SITTING in his office for an hour, a phone call finally came through to Biz and because Doc was the only person who knew he was alive, he contemplated before answering. He wasn't sure if he was ready to hear the truth; either way it went, shit was complicated. If Bonnie was pregnant with his baby, without a doubt he was going to let her live, but the how aspect of how she was gonna live taunted him. He knew he couldn't whisk Bonnie away to a mansion like he had done Cyn, because he knew Bonnie would make a grand escape and most likely her and her brother would attempt to finish him off. So his only other option was to have her in his presence at all times. No one could keep an eye on her like he could. And if she wasn't pregnant, then that was it. Bonnie was dead and he didn't know if he could live with that neither. He and Bonnie had spent most of their time together and he had learned how to appreciate a woman. She had penetrated something within him that had died so long ago. And for some reason, he couldn't shake the feeling off and lock that beast back in its cage. Just as the phone was about to stop ringing, he answered and put it to his ear without saying a word. "It's positive brother; she's twelve weeks in."

"Possibility of paternity?"

"You about to be a pops nigga." A quick rush of happiness ran through his body as Doc beamed the results, happier for Biz than he was for himself. His rush of happiness left his body just as quick as it had come, and now Biz had to do what he had to do. The news caused him to finally build the courage to go back into the garage and tend to Bonnie. He had thought of just letting her stay there and rotting until death if she wasn't pregnant but now that he knew she was, he had to step his game up. He was pent up in the crib anyways and with Bonnie also there, he had to make sure he was safe in his own spot.

9

DECEIT

"Deceit's favorite role is playing the victim."

— PAUL E. GALINDO

*H*arper sat in front of her husband twiddling with her fingers, for the first time, nervous and scared of the man that she married. She didn't know if it was the veins that popped out from his neck and the middle of his forehead, or if it was because when she looked in his eyes, she didn't see the same Chris she had married. Basic ass Chris was gone, and this right here was Christopher. They had been sitting in silence and she knew there could only be one reason why he was as upset as he was. She had deceived him in the worst way, but how he found out, she had no idea, but she was sure to find out.

"Six years, six fucking years Harper!" he said, breaking the silence while trying to mentally calm himself, but to no avail; his anger was taking over. "Why? Just tell me why. Give me a reason good enough so I won't have to break your fucking neck." The sound of the malice in his voice caused a shiver to go up her spine. He had never spoken to her in this way and it did something to her. She could feel the hate in his voice and could only believe that he meant his threat. She wanted to panic but knew she couldn't. Chris stood at six feet and he was big enough to be a football player. There was no outrunning him or outdoing anything. Tears threatened to spill from her eyes and all she could think about was calling Bonnie. She would surely save her from this nightmare, but Bonnie was nowhere to be found. She had one other option, and that was Havoc, and calling out to him for help was a gamble. It was worth a shot.

She looked at the clock and it read 3:15 p.m. CJ's bus was gonna be pulling up to the house in any second. And she just hoped and prayed that she would be saved by him. She heard the horn to the bus beeping outside which signaled for a parent to come and get him, and Harper stood up and so did Chris. She tried to back away from him but her four steps back were nothing to his one step forward. He forcefully gripped her hair and pulled her head back. "I'm not fucking done with you! Get your fucking son, and imma deal with the both of you!" Harper didn't say a word. She let the tears that ran from her eyes speak for her. She didn't feel safe and knew that if she didn't get out of there that she would be circled in chalk.

The horn to the bus beeped again and this time, Chris pushed her towards the door causing her to stumble. She opened the front door and walked towards the bus knowing that Chris was burning a hole in her back. She pulled her phone out her front pocket, trying not to make it obvious, and quickly shot Havoc a text.

Harper: Help me please!!! NOW!! 911!!

She shoved the phone back in her pocket and forced a smile on her face when she got in the view of the bus driver. She leaned down and hugged her son tightly. "Aooow Mommy, you are squeezing too tight," he complained, and Harper pulled back and looked at him, admiring his features. Her baby's tannish skin color was what gave the secret away and she knew it. She just figured Chris loved her enough to look past her flaws, but little did she know Chris's ego was bruised like never before. "Daddy's home!" he squealed as he looked over his mother's shoulder and saw his father standing at the door. Harper wanted to yank him back by his bookbag, but she was too late when CJ began sprinting towards the only man he knew as his dad. She watched as Chris absentmindedly greeted CJ telling him to go up to his room, without moving his eyes off of Harper. She wanted to scream and shout for help, but CJ was already in the house and she didn't want anything to happen to him. She walked back towards the house hoping that Havoc would come to her rescue. He was her only chance and she knew it. The minute she got into the house, Chris's fist came crashing towards her face dislocating her jaw. She slid down on the floor wincing, trying to not make too much noise. She didn't want CJ to witness whatever it was Chris was about to do to her.

"You lied to me for six fucking years about that fucking nigger being my boy! I'm going to ask you once Harper, is he mine?" Without giving her a chance to speak, he pulled a paper out of his pocket and opened it up. "Possibility of paternity, ZERO." He crumbled up the paper and kneeled down and grabbed her by her jaw and squeezed, causing her to wince as her mouth opened and he shoved the paper in. "You're a sneaky, lying, conniving slut bitch," he spewed while standing up to his feet pacing back and force. "I should've known, I should've fucking known. But I gave you the benefit of the doubt. But once that little motherfucker's skin began to turn tan, I knew it! I knew it! Look at me! And look at you! Am I tan? Are you fucking tan? No, we are whiter than fucking clouds! So not only did you fucking cheat with a nigger, you had a fucking mullato baby! I should kill you! Matter of fact, I AM going to kill you." He began walking toward the kitchen and Harper wanted to just run out the door but with the way Chris was talking, she was sure he'd kill her son. She tried to dash towards the steps but once again, the number of steps she were able to take with her short legs were no more than the few steps Chris took with his long legs and grabbed her by her hair. And she felt the cold steel from the knife against her neck.

She closed her eyes and before she knew it, her door came crashing down startling Chris, which made him loosen his grip on her giving her the advantage to jet up the stairs. Havoc stood there and after giving one look at Harper, he pulled the trigger allowing a bullet to go into Chris's side and one in his leg.

"Ahhhhh, Harper! Stop him! Please!" Chris begged, as if the shoe were on the other foot he would be at her mercy. Harper wanted to let Havoc end him, but she couldn't live with his death being on her conscience. She just wanted out.

"Don't kill him, please," Harper said in a little above a whisper just as Havoc had taken a step forward and aimed at his head. He thought about killing him anyways and Harper knew it. She rushed back down the steps and touched Havoc's hand forcing him to put his hand down. "Just get me out of here Rashad, please," she pleaded, looking him in his eyes. And he nodded his head without looking at her.

"If you say a word about this to anyone, I will find you and kill you. Harper won't be able to save you then. If you touch or come near her, or her son, I will kill everyone that you love without a thought. They call me Havoc for a reason, and I don't think you wanna find out why, nigga." Chris nodded his head as fear took over him. The two bullets that Havoc had put in him already let him know that he wasn't playing and would stick to his promise. It was as if anger and fear were one the way it switched in Chris.

Harper rushed up the stairs into her son's room grabbing a suitcase from under his bed and stuffing clothes inside. "Mommy, where are we going?" CJ asked curiously taking his eyes off of his Nintendo switch.

"We are going to stay with Uncle Rara, for a while papa. Pack everything you want to bring with you in here," she said once she finished putting all his clothes inside the bag. Without giving him a chance to respond, she rushed to her room and grabbed her bag from under her bed and did the same. She just wanted to get out the house in one piece. She grabbed her bag off the bed once she was done and walked past the mirror noticing her swollen jaw. Her adrenaline had been rushing so much she didn't even realize how much pain she was really in.

She rushed back into CJ's room attaching his bag to hers and lifting him up in her arms. CJ was half of her body length already but right now, she didn't care. She was trying to get the hell out of dodge. "Alright CJ listen, close your eyes and no peeking. Uncle Rara wanted to surprise you, so when I say open, you open your eyes and act surprised to see him, okay?" CJ chuckled and nodded his head, listening to his mother. He covered his eyes and squeezed them shut as Harper began to walk with him in her arms and down the steps. Havoc stood at the bottom of the step as Chris laid in pain as blood seeped out of him. "Apply pressure," Harper said, still showing that she cared for her husband. Havoc grabbed the bags from her and followed her out closing the door behind her. "Alright CJ, on the count of three open your eyes," Harper said while putting him down. "One...two...three!"

CJ peeled his hands off his face and pretended to be surprised seeing

Havoc standing there as he ran over to him and jumped in his arms. Havoc held him up as confusion plagued him and Harper wanted to laugh but she couldn't. She had broken her own heart and marriage. There was no turning back and CJ didn't even know it. She didn't know how she would tell him and wasn't prepared to tell him. She jumped in the car while Havoc strapped CJ in and took a seat in the driver's side. She pushed her chair back and took a deep breath, trying to calm her nerves. She wanted to cry so bad but not in front of CJ. She knew the questions would start and she didn't have an answer for them. At least not right now.

Havoc could see how troubled she was, and he cursed himself right now. If Bonnie were here, he wouldn't be dealing with this right now and it was going on two weeks since he'd last heard from his sister. He knew she wasn't dead, he could feel it. But nothing was coming up and every end of his search was a dead end. "Have you spoken to B?" he asked like he did every day, texting Harper to see if maybe she had. Harper shook her head as thoughts of Bonnie filled her head as well. She had questions and she knew the only person who could give her answers was Havoc.

"Is she dead?" she said, barely over a whisper so CJ couldn't hear her. Havoc shook his head from side to side.

"Nah, she's good."

Harper opened her eyes and looked at him this time as he drove without taking his eyes off the road. "How do you know?"

"Twin telepathy," he responded plain and simple.

MINI-ME

"Without a positive male role model in your life, it is extremely difficult to become a man who benefits his family and benefits society."

— DONALD MILLER

"*N*inety-one, ninety-two, ninety-three." Havoc watched as his apprentice Ivory counted, finishing up his one hundred push-ups. Ivory was thirteen and the streets were raising him. Both of his parents had been killed when he was five and since he'd turned eight, the system had done a bad job on keeping track of him.

Havoc had found the young boy three years prior sleeping behind a dumpster and took him under the wing. He even had him set up in a mini studio apartment for himself. Havoc knew what it was like to grow up without parents so when he looked at Ivory, he saw the younger version of himself. Except he had always had Bonnie. Ivory was literally all alone, no parents nor siblings. Havoc let him come and go as he pleased but always made sure he was good. With all the bad that he did in the world, taking Ivory in was the one good thing that he was doing. Havoc was as open with Ivory as Bonnie was with Harper and he didn't hold back. He had schooled the young boy on life, drugs, women and getting money. And to Ivory, Havoc's word was godly. He knew about what Havoc did for a living and wanted to be just like him. He felt like he owed Havoc his life and the only way that he could pay his debt to him was to show him that he was ready to kill.

What Ivory didn't know was that Havoc was in no rush. He had trained the boy for three years and if he told Ivory jump, he'd ask how high. Havoc knew that Ivory's loyalty was to him and Ivory showed him that, time and time again. Ivory didn't speak of Havoc to any of the people he knew in these streets. Ivory kept Havoc up on game on what was going on. He was Havoc's eyes and ears and for that alone, he was compensated nicely. Whereas all the other young boys on the strip were slanging drugs to keep up with the older cats, Ivory was keeping his hands clean just as Havoc had told him. The boys on the block wondered how he could afford the clothes on his back and the fly kicks he wore daily, but Ivory never told them a thing. He just watched them and cracked jokes and told them mind they business. "I'm done man. When are we gonna get into the real action though? Working out is cool and all. Shit, I'm the only thirteen-year-old on the block that look like Vin Diesel. Them niggas wish they could get ock like me," Ivory stated while grabbing his bottle of water and rag off the floor while flexing in the mirror. Havoc looked at him, raised an eyebrow and shook his head. He had no doubt in his mind that Ivory was ready and that was why he was about to give him what he was asking for all this time.

In three years, Havoc had sculpted Ivory's mind keeping him head strong. A strong mind meant nothing when one had a weak heart and Havoc had trained him on that as well. He had penetrated the depths of Ivory's brain the way Biz had done he and Bonnie. He had shown Ivory how to survive in these streets without him. Once a month he had locked Ivory out his apartment for an entire week forcing him to kick in his survival mode and Ivory had mastered it. Without Havoc, Ivory would still be able to hold his own and that was all Havoc wanted. "You think you ready Ivy?"

As if he could show him better than he could tell him, Ivory got back onto the floor in push-up position. Putting a hand behind his back, he began to push up and down while looking Havoc dead in his eyes, unfazed. Even throwing in a yawn to show him how ready he was. "You don't think I'm ready?" Ivory asked back.

Havoc leaned forward in his chair eyeing his protégé; he knew he was ready. He was ready a year ago, but Havoc wanted to know that he wanted it. Him knowing consisted of more than Ivory just begging him every other day. His actions needed to show that he wanted it. Because once he was in, he was in, and he would be labeled as a killer. He didn't want to get Ivory's head too big, that's why he never told him he was ready, but tonight he would be able to prove himself. "We'll see. I got a name and a place for you. The rest is on you," he said while standing up. Ivory stood to his feet eager to show Havoc that all that he had been doing wasn't for nothing. That he was ready, born ready for this moment. "Strength doesn't come—"

"From what you can do. It comes from overcoming the things you once thought you couldn't," Ivory cut him off, stating what Havoc had told him consistently for the past three years. "I'm ready. I won't let you down."

"Aight, meet me at the crib at 7:45 p.m.," Havoc said before turning to walk away.

* * *

HAVOC WALKED into his house and he could hear Harper and CJ in the backyard. She had been staying at his place for a week now. She felt safe with Havoc. With Bonnie not being around and not knowing exactly where she was, she didn't want to stay at her home alone. She hadn't heard from Christopher since she left their house and was happy but somewhat sad. CJ had begun asking questions about his dad on the second day of being at Havoc's house, and Harper had lied saying that he had went on a business trip. It wasn't unlikely for Chris to go on a business trip. He had gone on plenty and CJ was aware of it. But his questions didn't end there. He went on to ask why they were at Uncle Rara's house and how long they'd be there, not that he actually minded though. He was just six and nosey. He loved Uncle Rara's house; with the big backyard and pool, it was almost as fun as being at a water park. Harper rarely took CJ to swim but it was good to see that those swimming lessons had paid off. She sat at the edge of the pool with her feet in the water as CJ swam back and forth jumping off the diving board. She was comfortable in Havoc's home and knew they couldn't stay forever. She had the money to get a place but she just hadn't gotten around to it. With being a single mom and working, she had barely any time to herself.

Havoc wasn't used to having a woman and kid in his home. And it wasn't as bad as he thought it would be. CJ brought life into his home, and he felt a connection to the boy. He knew a connection when he felt it and CJ was no stranger to him. The two had always gotten along well. The day Havoc had gotten Harper from her house he knew what the reason behind the fight was without her even telling him. It was clear as day that Chris wasn't CJ's dad but if that was a lie that Harper wanted to stick by, that was on her. Even Stevie Wonder could see the tanned skin that CJ had. His once quiet home was no longer quiet, and he wasn't sure how to feel about it. He walked to the screen door that led to the backyard and just stood there watching Harper toss CJ the ball as he tried shooting it in the hoop from the pool.

"Uncle Rara!! Come out here and play me! One on one," he shouted while getting out the pool and bouncing the ball before shooting it in the hoop. Havoc was impressed. Not many six-year-olds had the skill CJ had. *Yea, that boy's daddy is definitely black,* he thought to himself.

"You want me to school you CJ? Is that what you're asking?" Havoc said challenging the young boy, while catching the ball and shooting what would be a three-pointer.

"School me? Heck nah. If I win, I'll be your maid for the day. If you win, you take me for ice cream tomorrow."

Havoc stood back putting his hand to his chin, acting as if he was thinking about it. "Aight, bet. Game is ten." He passed the ball to CJ and began to play.

Harper stood to her feet and let them play their game as she walked into the house. Havoc had shown a side of him with CJ that she never knew existed. She had realized that she didn't really know him after all. The time she usually spent around him was when he popped in at Bonnie's and did some shit talking and left. He was always so serious and had never shown that he was even capable of smiling, but now Harper knew that was not true. She liked seeing him like this and she had noticed how beautiful a smile from him was. Havoc had interacted with CJ more than his actual father had. She watched from inside the screen door as Havoc swooped CJ up throwing him in the pool after he scored a shot and began boasting. The smile on CJ's face was why Harper was so thankful for Rashad. She began to chuckle as CJ got back out the pool and tried pushing Havoc in and he played along, getting right into the pool with all his clothes and sneakers.

He got out the pool and kicked his shoes off while pulling his shirt over his head. Harper couldn't help but to admire his body. His muscles were so perfectly built it was as if each muscle had been placed there individually. Hers eyes went down his body as the water did and she stared at his V-line and shook her head, taking her attention away from there and looking back up to his face only to see that he had caught her looking. She turned and walked away, embarrassed at getting caught, and her face turned bright red. Havoc shook his head and continued to play with CJ, wondering after all if having Harper and CJ around was a good idea.

* * *

AT 7:00 P.M. Havoc got a text to his phone.

Ivy: Open up.

He rose from the couch and walked over to the door and Ivory stood there in all-black attire. Just as Havoc had told him previously, Ivory had to work his way up to white collar crime, where he had to wear a suit and tie, but what he had on right now was perfect. "If you're early you are on time, if you are on time you are late," he spoke, letting Havoc know that he had been soaking up every word he had been saying for the past few years.

Havoc stepped off to the side and let Ivory in and led him into the basement. The basement was where Havoc now conducted his business. He had swiftly taken over Biz's business and questions were beginning to be asked by his peers, and he didn't like it. Feeling like they would be a problem, he made it a mission to take them out one by one, and with Ivory's help. If Ivory could take out his colleague swiftly, then he would know one hundred percent sure that he was ready. Everyone's loyalty was to Biz in this game and he knew he had to build it from the ground up just as Biz had done. He walked into the small part of the basement where everything looked normal, before punching in a code and the wall slid to the side letting him into the main part. Ivory looked on in surprise as he saw all the weapons and arsenal Havoc had on his wall, along with deadly liquids and pills all labeled to perfection. Havoc was exactly what Ivory wanted to be and he wanted to show him that. And tonight, he would prove it to him. The door closed automatically behind them as Havoc walked over to his file cabinet that held all the information of every hit and every person who worked for Dead Silence. After comparing kills, he realized that Bonnie had the most of them. Bonnie. His twin sister was out there somewhere, and he had no clue where. He had put his search for her on hold. She was him and he knew she was making it work. He pushed Bonnie to the back of his head as he thought about the task at hand.

"This is the last step of your training. You have eight kills then once you execute them all, I'll know you're ready," Havoc said grabbing the first file out and tossing it to Ivory. He took a seat behind his desk as Ivory took a seat in front, opening the file and taking in all the information. He had given Ivory one of the easiest of them all to kill, Ray. Ray was good at what he did, but the money, the bottles and bitches kept him distracted. It was a flaw of his that Biz hated and knew would cause his demise. And little did he know, Havoc thought the same. Ray kept the same routine on a Saturday night. He didn't miss a moment to be at the club.

"This is it?" Havoc nodded his head before raising up out his seat and walking to what he called his wall of death.

"Pick your poison," he offered, but Ivory shook his head and lifted his shirt revealing his 9 mm and pulled a silencer out his pocket and screwed it on.

"Imma make this quick and easy," he replied with a smile. Havoc rose his hands in surrender taking two steps back. He was proud of what Ivory had become and knew that he would be one of the biggest assets to his company.

He walked out the basement with Ivory on his tail leading him to the front door. He let Ivory out and turned to head up the stairs to his bedroom to get dressed.

Ivory thought he'd be handling things all on his own and Havoc wanted him to believe that. He was going to tail him and be his second pair of eyes to see how Ivory operated and make sure that he was good.

After all, he was going after the smoothest assassins in the city. He threw on gear that was similar to Ivory's, if not the exact same, before tucking his gun in his waistband. He stepped out the bedroom and collided into a wet Harper. The towel wrapped around her chest and wet hair was confirmation that she had just gotten out the shower

"I'm...I'm so sorry," she said avoiding eye contact with him and grabbing on her towel for dear life as if it would walk off her body. Havoc nodded his head before walking around her and heading out the door leaving Harper standing there sulking in his scent.

Havoc sat in his car in a back alley where he had a view of the club. He watched as Ivory stood beside the dumpster. After about thirty minutes, Ray was walking out by himself. Ivory scoped the area seeing that there were a few people standing out front, and he also knew that if he didn't get Ray now that he would have to wait another week if Havoc allowed him. This was his shot and he had to prove himself. Just as he began to walk from behind the dumpster disguising himself as a young bum, Ray began to walk to the back.

"I gotta piss, shit," Ray said, before going to where Ivory had just been standing, and began unzipping his jeans. A wide smile spread across Ivory's face as he pulled his gun out his pocket and let two rounds go in the back of Ray's head before walking off and not looking back.

Havoc looked on to see if anyone had seen anything, but everyone seemed to be so engaged with what they were doing that they didn't even realize that a murder had been committed right before them.

BONNIE AND CLYDE

"The new Bobby and Whitney. Only time we don't speak is during *Sex and the City*."

— JAY- Z

*I*t had been three weeks of being cooped up in the house with Biz, and Bonnie no longer felt like a prisoner. Although he had hidden every sharp object around, she didn't want to escape. Being in his presence alone was enough for her. She had killed so much that living a regular life was almost impossible and now here in this house held captive with her child's father, she felt this was regular and she enjoyed it. The two didn't speak no more than two sentences to one another and Bonnie was ready to break the ice. Biz just thought any conversation between them would complicate things and Bonnie couldn't see it. She had lost her first love and managed to love again thinking that she lost him, but she was adamant about not letting him slip through her fingers again.

She stood by the window in the bedroom that she was locked in and just focused on the view as she thought up a plan to get close enough to Biz again to try and get him to trust her again. She walked over to the intercom on the wall that he had installed so no matter where he was around the house, she could read him.

"We need to talk," was all she said, keeping it short and simple. Enough to peak his curiosity.

Biz stopped mid sit up as he heard Bonnie's voice go through the intercom. Little did she know, her voice to him was like music and the distance he kept between them was what he felt was best. He didn't want to backtrack. They could never be. Her brother would never allow them to be, not that Biz cared but he knew Bonnie did. He had thought his plan through on how to kill Havoc, but she was the one stopping him. The thought of him possibly losing her behind it meant losing his access to his child, and it was a risk he was contemplating on taking.

He rose up from the ground and grabbed his rag, wiping the sweat that had formed from his workout on his forehead, before taking steps two at a time to her room. He used the key that locked the bedroom door from the outside and opened it up, and right in front of him stood a naked Bonnie.

"Come on B, fuck is you doing?" he asked looking away from her, but his facial expression not changing. Pregnancy was doing her body right. She was gaining weight in all the right places and it was something he realized but didn't want to make known that he realized. But here Bonnie stood naked as the day she was born, and he wanted to swoop her up into his arms and have her in the worst way, but he knew he couldn't.

"I want to talk."

His eyes were now at her feet where he located her robe at and without a word, he walked over to her causing her to take two steps back. He paused in his step after realizing that he had instilled fear in her. He bent down and picked up the robe opening it up for her to step into it. "I ain't gone hurt you," was all he said after stepping back. She closed her robe and took a seat on the edge of her bed, patting beside her for him to sit and he declined. "I'll stand, let's talk. Wassup?"

"I want to come out the room. I won't try no funny business. If I do, you can lock me in here till I give birth. Just trust me, please."

Biz looked at her as if she had grown three heads and scoffed. "Trust? Trust who? You hear yourself ma? Last time I trusted you I got this and this!" he said pointing at his scar on his chest and on his forehead. Trust you? Never again." The silence in the room was thick and although

Bonnie was a tough bitch, this pregnancy was turning her soft and she was sure of it the minute tears began to fall from her eyes. She quickly wiped them away hoping that Biz didn't see but little did she know, he realized everything about her. From her barely there bulge in her belly to the glow in her skin from pregnancy. But of course, she didn't think he paid that much attention to her.

"If you can't let me come out can you spend time with me? I feel like a fucking prisoner in here. No, scratch that, prisoners have more freedom than I do. All I see all fucking day are these four walls, and it's driving me crazy. I just need someone to talk to from time to time. Can you do that?" she asked, feeling defeated. She knew that things weren't just going to go her way. She had to take baby steps to gain Biz's trust back.

Biz thought about what she was asking and wanted to decline, but it was the least he could do. He didn't trust her, and it wasn't like he was going anywhere or speaking with anyone in the outside world anyways. So, keeping Bonnie company would be a breeze for him, at least that's what he thought. He nodded his head, giving in to her, before standing on his own two feet. "Imma get in the shower, have Burke chef us up some food and I'll be back," he said before walking out the room and leaving the door unlocked. Bonnie had realized that he had left the door unlocked and stared at it, wondering if he'd done it on purpose trying to test her. But like she made clear before, she didn't want to escape. Being here with Biz gave her the normalcy that she had wanted in her life for so long. She had lived what she thought was normal through Harper. And now there was no Harper.

She stood up contemplating going to the door just to get some fresh air around the house and just thought against it. Biz didn't trust her, and she knew if she did that then he would only confirm his own suspicions. She walked straight into the bathroom and stood in the mirror looking at her growing hair. Her pregnancy had her skin glowing, hair growing and booty fatter, and she was loving every bit of it. She turned to her side to see her bump and still her stomach was flat. She couldn't believe that she was three months and still not showing. She put it in her mind that the next time she saw Doc she would ask questions. She turned the shower on and stepped in, letting the water caress her hair and body. *Imma get my man back*, she thought to herself as she thought of all the tricks she had up her sleeve to win Biz back. She had never been dismissed by a man and being that she had so much time on her hands, chasing Biz was a mission for her. Having him was key. Biz had her smitten and he had no idea. Her love for him had surpassed her love for Khalil, and she wanted to make sure he knew it from her actions.

She washed her body and hair, wishing that it was Biz's hand caressing her body instead of her own, before stepping out and drying off. She had her mind set on throwing on a black lace lingerie, and rubbed coconut all over her body and hair as well before stepping out the bathroom. When she stepped back in her room a tray was sitting on her bed and she was waiting on Biz to come back. To occupy her time she turned to the vanity mirror putting on a light gloss coating on her lips and brushing her eyebrows. She was in need of getting pampered, her eyebrows needed doing and her hair did as well. She looked at the clock and it felt like she'd been waiting on Biz for an hour but only fifteen minutes had passed. She let out a deep breath as her stomach began to grumble and walked over to the tray of food. The aroma was calling out to her and she was ready to see what it was. The minute she sat on the bed and touched the top to reveal her food, Biz came in and stared at her. She looked up at him, looking into his eyes trying to read him, but nothing. "It's about time you came. I'm starving, come on have a seat," she said while about to reveal their food, but Biz walked over to her stopping her hand. She looked up at him confused and with a slight attitude this time. She was ready to eat, and she had waited for him long enough.

He grabbed her hand, standing her up and grabbing the tray off the bed. "Let's go," he said, leading her out the room, and she stopped in her tracks wondering if he was playing some kind of trick on her. But with every step that he took farther and farther away from the room, she realized that he was serious. She slid her feet in her paw slippers before retreating out the room and following the scent of the food to where Biz was. He sat seated at the head of a long, rectangular, oak table and she sat where her food had been placed at the other end.

The two began to eat without saying a word. This was not how Bonnie wanted it, but it was how Biz needed it so that they didn't cross that thin line that wandered between the both of them. "What made you change your mind?"

"If you wanted to leave you would've left. I gave you the opportunity whether you knew it or not and you're still here. So, the least I can do is let you walk around freely."

"I told you I'm not leaving, I like being here. I just would like to see more of you," she stated while stuffing her mouth with a piece of lobster. She couldn't deny the fact that she ate good every day. Every day, Biz's personal chef Burke cooked a flavorful gourmet meal, and Bonnie couldn't deny that he knew what he was doing when he was in the kitchen. "I thought you were dead," she added, and sadness overcame her.

"I thought I was too ma. You did a nigga dirty."

"Let me prove myself to you. Trust isn't given but it's earned. Let me earn that trust back Biz."

Biz put his fork down and put his hands together looking her directly in her eye. He wanted to believe her, but he didn't know. He was looking to see if he could recognize any type of foul play in her but was coming up short. The sincerity in her eyes matched the sincerity in her voice. "Let's take it a step at a time. You are free to come and go as you please around the house. Do not attempt to leave Bonnie," he warned, laying it all on the table. She had six more months before birth and although he didn't trust her, he didn't want her to go crazy.

A smile crept on Bonnie's face and Biz looked away. That smile was enough for him to throw everything off the table and have her for dinner, but of course he opted against it. "I won't."

When they both finished eating, Bonnie grabbed her dishes and walked over to Biz's grabbing his and taking them to the sink and washing them. She took in the surroundings of the entire house and it was nothing more than she expected. The house was fit for a king and to her, that was what Biz was. A King. And she was gonna do what she had to do to be his queen. Biz stared at her ass for a few seconds and what he wanted to do was tell her fuck them dishes and bend her over and lick every part of her body. But that wasn't happening. Not now, not ever. Bonnie wasn't gonna reel him in again like she had done previously.

He stepped into the living room putting on CNN. Since he was cooped up in the house just as much as Bonnie, the news had become his best friend. It was how he now stayed in tune with what was going on in the outside world.

"BREAKING NEWS: Four men and two women killed in the past week. Police have reason to believe that this was gang related being that each person killed all have the same matching tattoo of a skull. Although each person shows no other connection besides a skull, police still think that it is gang affiliated. I'm Adrian Bailey and you are watching FOX 5."

A flame lit up inside of Biz after hearing the news report. He sat back in his seat and Bonnie took a seat beside him and the same thoughts ran through both of their heads as Biz propped her foot on his lap and rubbed her skull tattoo, and she placed her hand on his where his tattoo resided. The news and the police had no clue what they were talking about, but Bonnie and Biz knew that it had Havoc written all over it. "He's taking over," Bonnie said breaking the silence. Biz nodded his head and stood to his feet as the anger that began to consume him showed. He had built his organization from the ground up and here Havoc was trying to make it into his. Biz had sat back and let shit die down but this right here, he wasn't standing for. He had to think up a plan and fast.

"That's my shit he tryna take over! You want me to trust you? Show me that you down for a nigga," he proposed while looking Bonnie in her eyes. She knew this was her moment to prove herself, but what he was asking was to turn against her flesh and blood. It had been almost a month and Havoc hadn't done a thing to look for her, and that alone was enough to make her take up Biz on his offer.

"I'm down," she said without giving it any more thought. Havoc had shown her that he would kill her for any affiliation with Biz, and she didn't like it. He had made it clear after he put his hands on her when he was suspecting her pregnancy and gave her enough reasons to want to go against him. Biz, on the other hand, had spared her life. Although she didn't ask Biz what was next, she knew he wanted Havoc's head on a platter and just hoped that she would be able to deliver.

He walked away without saying another word. This was the ultimate test for Bonnie. He had given her an ultimatum and she had chosen him, and now it was time to see if she could stand by her word. Because she was pregnant, he had time to plan things through. Bonnie remained in her seat knowing that once Havoc found out she went against the grain that she would have no other choice but to kill him. As Biz began to think of his own plan to put in effect, Bonnie thought of her own. Havoc was no dummy and there needed to be some kind of bulletproof plan that he couldn't see through. Yea, Biz's plan may have been good, but nobody knew her twin brother the way she did and only she knew how high up his guards were. So whether Biz knew it or not, Bonnie's part of the plan was needed.

Bonnie stared at the tattoo of the skull that had her own personal touch of her favorite flower daffodils for eyes. She remembered the day she got it. Every member of Dead Silence adorned their own personal skull tattoo wherever they wanted it and however they wanted it. It was almost like a tattoo to get sworn into the organization. The day Bonnie had gotten hers, she felt like she was on top of the world and that nothing could stop her or get in her way. The tattoo was who she was and she loved everything about it. Dead Silence had saved her and created her into the woman she was today. And although Havoc was her brother, she was loyal to Biz. Had it not been for him, she knew she wouldn't be where she was today. Biz had molded them and protected them, showing them how to fend for themselves, something people rarely did. In her mind, Biz had fucked up. He had chosen money over his own people but he wasn't to blame. This was all business and the person to blame was the one who put out the hit. Thoughts rummaged through her mind about who could have wanted Khalil dead. He was just like her. Came from nothing and taken in by Biz. She and Khalil were thick as thieves, closer than her and Havoc had ever been. She knew everything about him, so she thought. This hit was so out of the blue for her and it never sat well with her. So as she put out a mission to help Biz take Havoc out, she needed for Biz to help her find out who put the hit out on Khalil. She wanted to prove her loyalty to both of the men that she loved in her lifetime, even if it meant disregarding the life of her brother.

1 2

HAPPY DEATH DAY

"I think being vulnerable, paves the way for humility."

— JOHNATHAN SADOWSKI

*B*enny Lays sat at a table with four of his other business partners. At the table, he out of the four held the most weight, and although it was never proven, many had suspected him to own the Dead Silence organization. Rumor had it that Benny took care of all the major hits in the streets but that's all they were, rumors. Kingpin by day and assassin by night, Benny never denied or confirmed the allegations. It kept his comrades on their toes about him which gave him the upper hand. He simply went with the flow. The more that people thought that, the more that they didn't cross him, and it was something that made his life a little more easier.

"Daddy, Daddy, can you please get into the pool with me?" his four-year-old daughter Beatrice pleaded as she tugged on his arm with a slight pout on her face. Today was her day and it was Benny's job to cater to her.

"Of course, Bee, tell your mother to put on your swimsuit before she decides it's time to cut your cake," he responded while pointing at his wife who was unpacking a Minnie Mouse cake. It was Bee's fourth birthday party and Benny was doing it big with a pool party like he did every year. He spared no expense on this one day of the year, with the bouncy castles, the clowns walking around making children balloon animals, face painting, cotton candy machines, and snow cone machines were all in attendance. This was the most normal day of Benny's life. The most accessible day he would call it. The catered food and the few guests of business partners and whatever family his wife invited were all in attendance.

Benny never invited people into his home. He was one of the most lethal cats in these streets and the life he led wasn't meant for a family, but of course shit happened. He had fallen in love and created a family, and it was his responsibility to take care of them every step of the way making sure nothing happened to them. Biz had warned every single person he employed that having a family wasn't wise, but had also taught them to stay on their toes in case it happened. So here Benny was, on his toes 24/7 sleeping with one eye open being the guard dog to his own home. Only on this one day of the year were people invited into his home. His daughter's birthday was the only day that he didn't have his guard up. Bee was so used to seeing her father so serious and all about his business at all times that he felt that he owed this day to her. Every year she looked forward to her party just so he could cater to her and be the dad she wanted him to be at all times. "Alright gentlemen, you heard the little lady. Tomorrow we are back to business. Today just sit back, relax and have a couple of margaritas and mimosas, as my wife would say," Benny said chuckling and waving one of the waiters over who had a tray of drinks. He grabbed a glass and downed it before running and jumping into the pool doing a cannonball, splashing some of the guests and making the kids get overly excited. His comrades sat back and chuckled, seeing a side of Benny that they barely ever saw. Bee jumped into the pool after her father looking down into the water, playfully thinking that he would swoop her up in his arms and throw her down into the water. But Bee was wrong. After a few seconds of him not coming up, she herself swam under the water after him. Panic set in her after realizing that her father wasn't moving, and that in fact her father had sunk to the bottom and his eyes were closed.

"Help!!" she shrieked out at the top of her lungs when she got back out the water. "Help my daddy!" Her little screams caused guests to begin gathering around after realizing what Bee had discovered. This gave Ivory the perfect opportunity to slip into the house and out the front door. He had just committed his last kill, the hardest kill of them all. What Benny thought was a mimosa was in fact mixed with chloroform. Ivory hopped on his bike that sat on the next block and went on his merry little way. He had bodied every person Havoc had given him and with each kill, it got harder and harder. But to him it was as if after every kill he felt like he was entering another level of *Call of Duty*. Benny had been saved for last and it had taken Ivory three weeks to actually pull it off. Havoc had sat back and let Ivory do things his way after the fourth kill, realizing that he had things under control. Nobody had suspected Havoc behind the hits because he had gotten word out to the rest of them that Bonnie was dead as well. His plan had been executed flawlessly and now the organization was his.

Ivory parked his bike on the side of Havoc's house before ringing the bell. "Nigga what the fuck do you got on?" Havoc asked as soon as he opened the door eyeing Ivory's waiter disguise. Ivory shrugged his shoulders before walking in. He unbuttoned his shirt revealing his chest.

"Call the tatt man up! I want my shit right here!" Ivory spoke excitedly. He had proven himself and now it was time for him to get his tattoo.

Havoc shook his head while leading him to the basement. "Ain't no more tatts nigga. That's that weak shit Biz was into. I got something better. Some shit that's forever." Ivory rose his eyebrow in confusion. He didn't have a single tattoo on his body and a tattoo at thirteen seemed like some fly shit. He couldn't understand what circles Havoc was speaking in.

"No offense, but fuck is better than a tattoo? We gon' be walking around with matching charm bracelets?" Ivory spoke up with a bit more frustration in his voice than he intended. Havoc just smiled. Ivory was hungry and he knew it. He walked over to his desk and pulled out a customized, stainless steel skull with a handle on it and passed it to Ivory. Ivory's eyebrows furrowed together as Havoc came from around his desk and went into a medicine cabinet that sat alongside his wall of death pulling out two muscle relaxers.

"Have a seat," Havoc instructed while walking out and into the smaller part of his basement, grabbing a bottle of brandy and a cup. The confused look on Ivory's face seemed to amuse him. He poured some brandy into the cup and handed the cup and the pills to Ivory. "Take that." He grabbed a blow torch off of his wall of death and turned it on using an automatic fire setting before grabbing the skull piece from Ivory. Biz had made everyone affiliated get the same tattoos and now that Havoc was running things it was gonna be slightly different.

Ivory had proved that he wanted to be down since day one and Havoc had molded him into the perfect killer. The last step was always the hardest. It was gonna be the body brand that was now going to be Dead Silence's symbol. Havoc had always thought that tattoos were too easy. As you can see, there were a million people in the world with them. But a body brand, only a select few had. To Havoc, the brand was proving loyalty to Dead Silence and all its people, something Biz had failed to do. There were many ways that he didn't agree with how Biz ran the company and just sat back and didn't say a word. And it took for Khalil to die for him to finally take a stand. He held the skull piece under the fire as Ivory watched him. For the first time, his instincts told him to run from Havoc, but his pride and loyalty kept him right where he was. He had committed all those kills and it couldn't be for nothing. *How bad could it be?* he thought. It was this one last step and he was ready to get it done and over with. He watched as the skull began to get bright red and closed his eyes as Havoc began walking towards him with it. "This shit is better than matching charm bracelets Ivy, don't you think?" Havoc said, chuckling before bringing the skull down onto Ivory's skin.

"AHHHHHHHHHHHHHHHHHHHHHHHHHHHHHHHHHHHH!!" Ivory yelled at the top of his lungs, passing out in the process. Havoc just shook his head and laughed. Whether Ivory knew it or not, Havoc had a newfound respect for him. He, at thirteen, had accomplished shit grown men couldn't do, endured pain that made grown men scream for their mama. He didn't know it, but he was second in line in Dead Silence.

Just like that, Havoc had given up Bonnie's spot in the organization. He hadn't seen her in a month and a half and he knew she was alive. He knew Bonnie was alive and well and if she hadn't reached out it was because she didn't want to, and the realization of that pissed him off. He knew his sister well enough to know that she knew when and how to get herself out of a sticky situation. They had always been able to sense when something was wrong with one another so he knew his instinct wasn't wrong. He had pushed Bonnie to the back of his mind because he had a business to run. If she wanted to play hide and seek, he wouldn't be around for it. Every day there were more wire transfers of money, photos and names. And although one couldn't see it, he was drowning in money. The organization had quickly gone from 10 to 2. The money was lovely and once Ivory touched it, he would know that everything that he had done was worth it.

After removing the steel from Ivory's skin, the brand looked just as Havoc had suspected it to look. It was a little swollen, per usual, but it was nothing that some ointment and a bandage wouldn't take care of, and he had the perfect person to do it. He rushed up the stairs quickly and nudged Harper who was sitting on a bar stool. "I need you to bandage something real quick," he said before turning around and walking away. Harper's curiosity had definitely peaked. She rushed up the stairs to the bedroom she stayed in and grabbed her bandage wraps in different sizes, some scissors, tape, and ointment. She had no idea what Havoc wanted her to bandage but knowing him, it could've been anything. She rushed back down the stairs and peeked in at CJ in the living room as he sat in front of the TV hypnotized by *Motown Magic*. She followed Havoc down to the basement and when she saw Ivory laying there passed out with a skull brand, her eyes widened. To her, Ivory was a baby. She never questioned what business he and Havoc had going on, but she knew it couldn't be nothing good. Seeing his branded chest, her heart went out for him. He was only thirteen; the life Havoc was leading him into wasn't a life for kids. The thought of Havoc being a bad example for CJ crossed her mind and she knew she had to leave.

Havoc could see all the emotion on her now pink face, but he wasn't fazed by it. He watched as she rushed over to Ivory and tended to him how a mother would to her child. She put a cream on his chest before wrapping him up and couldn't help herself when she kissed Ivory on the forehead. She just felt like he had needed it and there was no one else around to give it to him. When she was finally done, she cleared her throat and threw her shoulders back trying to keep her composure.

"Tomorrow I am going to start looking for a house," she stated, and Havoc just nodded his head not saying a word. He was almost sure that what he had just had her do, was what had her make that decision.

The two of them had become friends in the time that she had been living there and the bond that he built with CJ was breathtaking for him. He couldn't remember a time in his life where he felt as free as CJ felt, and it put a smile on his face. The thought of her moving was bittersweet. He had gotten a taste of what it was like to have a family and it wasn't as bad as he had imagined it. But Harper wanted to leave and who was he to ask her to stay. She wasn't his woman and maybe that was what he needed to stop himself from having dreams of her lips around his dick. Her leaving was more of a good thing than bad, he realized.

13

THE PERSON I USED TO KNOW

"There's something wrong with your character, if opportunity controls your loyalty."

— UNKNOWN

*H*arper walked around the condo that she'd been looking into and to her it was perfect. Two bedrooms for her and her baby boy. It was not too big and not too small. Their space was limited to one floor which was a change from what they were used to, but Harper didn't mind. As she looked around, she could picture the decorations on the walls and all around the house, and that alone made her comfortable. She knew that CJ would have questions. It seemed that he always had questions and she just didn't have all the answers. He had been asking about his father and Harper continued to tell him Daddy went away, and she didn't know when he'd be coming back. Now that they were moving to their own space, she could only imagine all the why questions he would have.

"What do you think about this one?" Jackie, her realtor, asked breaking up Harper's thought process.

"I think I'm gonna like it here," Harper said with a smile on her face.

"Alright then, to get this show on the road we need bank statements for proof of income, a copy of your ID, a security deposit of $1200 and first three month's rent which totals up to $3600."

Harper nodded her head before taking one more look at the place. "I'll have that all to you by the end of the week," she replied, and a wide smile spread across Jackie's face as she put her hand out to shake Harper's hand. Harper shook her hand as well before walking out.

The thought of her and CJ in their own space made her comfortable. She had loose ends to tie up with Chris and she was gonna deal with them today. She had been avoiding him and his phone calls, but now it was time to put what they had to rest.

She drove over to the place they had both once shared and all kinds of emotion came over her. In this house they had so many good memories, and the one bad memory there seemed to make all the good wash away like how water on a beach washed away footprints. Harper sat outside of what used to be her home for about thirty minutes before she built up the courage to get out. She opened up her glove compartment taking out a small piece that Havoc had given her for her protection and tucking it in her purse. The feel of a gun in the palm of her hands made them sweat. Her hands were shaky and all she was thinking to herself was that Chris didn't give her a reason to use it. She just wanted to get her divorce papers signed and be on her way. Was that too much to ask for?

After taking a deep breath and stepping out the vehicle, she used the key that she had and held onto her purse for dear life. To her, her life did depend on it. The only thing that could help her was this gun. She knew her petite frame was nothing compared to Chris's. She entered the house and all the mess that had been made was cleaned up. She wondered who exactly got it cleaned up but didn't think too hard on it. She entered the living room and the site before her caused her to loosen up on her bag. There was her husband sitting in a wheelchair without his legs and all kind of emotions ran through her. *Had she done this? Who was helping him? How was he getting himself cleaned up? What about food?* A million thoughts ran through her head before the final thought of *Why do you care?* entered her mind. But she knew deep in her heart it was because she loved Chris, she had made vows to him. She had made one simple mistake in their entire relationship and just thought they could get past it but instead, it backfired. Chris's stare that burned a hole in her almost made her forget the reason she had come over. "I see you finally built up the courage to make your grand fucking entrance," he said in a menacing tone, breaking the silence between them.

She cleared her throat and began to fumble in her bag looking for the papers, but also trying to be careful enough so that he wouldn't know that she had a gun. She didn't want to seem like the pathetic wife. She had done enough. He was wheelchair bound because of her, and that was enough. "I-I came here to bring you these," she stuttered. Something about him still made her intimidated. Chris had never put his hands on her prior to their incident, but that alone had instilled fear in her and he knew it. He enjoyed every minute of her fear. He began rolling his wheelchair and she began to take steps back. He chuckled because just as much as she had been contemplating on coming by to hand him these papers, he had been waiting to serve her with some information that he found out. He reached beside the TV and pulled out a folder and began to release all its contents onto the table.

"You see, after you and that bitch ass nigga cost me my legs, I have been having a lot of time on my hands considering the fact that I lost my job." He chuckled as if he was saying some kind of joke. "A lot of time on my hands is an understatement. I have too much damn time on my hands, and it's all thanks to you. Thanks to you, I have been able to dig up some dirt on the smart little neurosurgeon Dr. Leslie," he added, using her maiden name. He held up a highlighted bank statement and Harper stood, slightly confused at what he was getting at. She wanted to go closer to him but she wouldn't dare. "Before I get to this little artifact, I want you to know that I've been doing some deep digging. That pretty black bitch that seems so nice and fucking proper all the fucking time because she graduated Yale isn't who the hell I thought she was. See, I've always had my suspicions when it came to her because I've never met a smart ass negro. She almost had me fooled. All that is, is a ploy, a distraction, a disguise for what she really is. Is her name even really Bonnie? She had me fooled, but not anymore. That bitch is like the rest of those hoodlums. But she's good! She's good at hiding her true self. She should win a fucking Grammy, that's how good!" Harper began to get nervous. Chris had nothing to lose and the hate that he now harbored for his wife and Havoc was spreading like a fungus, and now Bonnie was a part of that hate train.

"How can I say this?" he asked rhetorically before spreading pictures of Havoc and Ivory across the table. "There's been a lot of killings going on and not too much surprise those niggers are behind it. I'm pretty sure you aren't surprised; for all I know, you're a part of them. You see, after your whoring cost me my legs and not being able to tell anyone how, I chose to hire a private investigator to spy on your friend Bonnie. I was going to seek my revenge through her and pump my dick down her throat. I'm pretty sure that black bitch would've liked it," he said chuckling. "But to my surprise, she has been MIA so my P.I. got sights on her brother hoping that he'd lead him to her but instead, he led him to a boatload of felonies." Harper's hands began to shake as she reached across the table and picked up the pictures, and she knew if they got in the hands of the law that Havoc and Ivory would be done. Ivory's life would be over before it even began.

"What do you want Chris? Why are you doing this?"

"Oh baby, I'm not even finished. This right here is the icing on the cake. Or should I say, it's the mother fucking cherry on top. You see, all I do is flip through magazines, sort through old mail and shred what we don't need. But I hit the lotto with this one. See, I've shredded a shit load of bank statements after opening them trying to see if you've been spending money on that nigger of yours, but what I found was much more juicy. This bank statement of a five-million-dollar wire transfer came and I couldn't wrap my head around why would a neurosurgeon have to wire transfer so much money. But I put two and two together and by the time I am done with you all, you all will be rotting in a jail cell and that fucking boy of yours will be getting fucked by the system."

Harper had heard enough and she knew that if she didn't act fast that Chris would stay true to his word. He did have too much time on his hands and he had figured out what she planned on taking to the grave with her. His revelation changed him from the man she once loved to her enemy. She couldn't risk her secret getting out and it was only one way to solve her problem. With sweaty hands, she dug in her purse and pulled out her small .9mm. Chris's eyes widened in surprise. He was right, Harper was now one of them and he was about to be the first kill she committed. "I'm sorry," she whispered before pulling the trigger three times, making sure they were all to his chest. It was twelve in the afternoon and she was sure all their neighbors were at work. But still, panic began to set in her. *What have I done?* she thought to herself. She pulled out her phone dialing the only person she felt could help her in this situation. She shoved the gun back into the purse and waited for his answer.

"Yo?"

"Please come by my house, I killed him. I need help," she said into the phone still shocked at her actions. She had used her hands to save so many lives and it seemed like this one kill had erased it all from her mind. *How could I? Who am I to decide that someone should live or die?* A million thoughts ran through her head as she began to pace with her hand on her forehead. *What if someone heard?* Her heart began to beat so fast she felt like it would fall out of her chest. *Maybe he's still alive. Three bullets? No way. He's dead. Let me check.* She debated with herself before raising her head up and looking at her dead ex-husband, whose head was now tilted back into his wheelchair. *He's dead,* she decided before going over to the curtains and closing them, making sure no one could see what was going on. She walked over to him, snatching the bank statement he held in his hand, and began rummaging through the folder that he held all his evidence in. Anything that was linked to her, she grabbed and turned on the shredder that once was in their bedroom but now resided in their living room. She began shredding all the papers he had on her and just as she put the bank statement through the shredder, she heard the front door open. She looked up startled and when she saw it was Havoc she let a breath out.

"I don't want to go to jail. Please help me." Havoc looked at Harper then at Chris wondering what the hell had happened, then his eyes went straight to the table. "He knew about you, Bonnie and Ivory. He was going to go to the police," she explained telling her half-truth, leaving the part about herself out. Havoc walked towards the table and picked up the pictures of he and Ivory in the act.

He looked up at Harper and what he used to see as "Bonnie's punk ass friend" was now looking like a ride or die. She had killed her own husband for him. She had proven her loyalty to him when he didn't ask. Her defending him made his dick hard. "What did you come here for?" he asked out of curiosity, trying to spot a lie in what she was saying. She picked up the papers that she had sat down on the table.

"I came to serve him these and he served me this," she explained. "So, are you going to help me?" she asked anxiously.

"I got it from here. Go back to the crib," he said, turning to face Chris, and shook his head. Harper was finally relieved. Bonnie had told her enough about the maids to know that they would get the job done.

She grabbed her purse and began to walk towards the door. She stopped in her tracks without turning around. "Thank you for everything. I found a place for CJ and I. We will be out by the end of the week."

14

LOVERS AND FRIENDS

"If we really want to love, we must learn how to forgive."

— MOTHER THERESA

*B*onnie stood in the floor-length mirror from the side looking to see if her flat belly had grown any. There was a slight bump that looked like she'd gotten it from eating but nope, that was her baby. She made four and a half months look good; she couldn't believe how well she was carrying. Every two weeks Doc had been coming by and checking the baby out and letting her know it was healthy and Bonnie couldn't be happier. Biz was still walking on eggshells around her but she was just happy to not be caged up in one room anymore and refused to give him a reason to lock her back in there. The thought of contacting Harper had crossed her mind a million times. She knew her friend was somewhere probably worried sick, but she just couldn't risk her freedom. It had been two months in a house with Biz and although they barely spoke, it felt good. She could see him admiring her when she walked past sometimes. Although he had never said it, she knew that deep down his feelings for her were mutual. He had let her in a bit when they first started fucking around and she fucked it up. She had already proven to him that she wouldn't try any funny business to leave and now today was the day she was going to try and take it up a notch.

"What time is Doc coming?" she asked while walking into the living room where he sat watching CNN. That seemed to be all he did these days. Havoc's reign was all over the news and Biz had figured out how to step in and handle him. He wasn't sure when, but he knew exactly how he'd do it.

"He should be here...now," he answered, looking at his clock, and like clockwork the bell rang. He looked up at Bonnie flashing her a small grin. He had no idea what something as small as a grin did to her. She walked over to the door greeting Doc and closing it behind her before going into the living room sitting on a reclining chair, anxious to hear her baby's heartbeat. "If you want to find out the gender, today is the day," Doc revealed. Bonnie began squealing, she couldn't wait. She hoped it was a little chocolate baby girl like herself so she could spoil her rotten.

"I hope it's a girl," she said, taking a deep breath and reclining back.

Biz could see she was excited, but he was about to burst her bubble like never before. "No gender, we will find out at birth," he stated sternly, and Doc nodded his head and Bonnie pouted her face.

"What the fuck do you mean no gender? I wanna know what the fuck my baby is," she said sitting back up, getting upset. Biz paid her no mind as he watched Doc put the gel on her stomach and do his thing. "Doc, I wanna know my baby's gender or this entire house going the fuck up in flames!" she threatened, but still nothing. She was getting more and more upset by the minute and Doc wouldn't budge to tell her the gender. After about twenty-five minutes, he finally stood up and gathered his things.

"Sorry B, you gon' be aight. Five more months to go and you'll be seeing what you're having," Doc said seeing Bonnie on the verge of tears. He and Bonnie had gotten comfortable with one another. After all, there wasn't anyone to talk to so when Doc came around, she made conversation and they joked here and there. They were no longer strangers to one another. Doc could tell that Bonnie had pull on Biz, but he didn't dare say a word unless Biz asked. He stayed in his place and that was it. After he got all his things together, Bonnie stood up and stomped all the way to the bedroom without saying a word.

When she was out of eyesight Biz cracked a smile and Doc shook his head. "Nigga you a clown," Doc said chuckling, realizing that Biz got a rise out of Bonnie and her attitude.

"She'll be aight, but yo, what we having?" he asked, and Doc looked at him with all seriousness wanting to know if he was serious. That caused Biz to chuckle. "I'm just fucking with you. Five months and we'll find out."

Doc shook his head once again and sat on the couch beside Biz. "What are you doing man? I usually just mind my business and come and go, but this ain't the regular Biz I'm used to, so tell me wassup."

"Man, imma keep it a buck with you. She got a nigga open. A nigga moving in ways that he ain't never moved before. I'm being all considerate and shit, doing shit I ain't never done before fam. No matter how much a nigga try to play it off, she's around and she gon' be around, but she don't know that. She don't need to know that. A nigga just gotta figure some shit out," he said, turning off the TV and running his hand through his dreads. Biz never really got frustrated but when thinking and talking about Bonnie, it seemed like all kind of frustration invaded him. He didn't recognize who he was when he was with her, and he knew it wasn't a good thing and just wanted to deal with her from a distance until he figured things out.

"Man, just remember who you are dealing with. Shorty is for you; I see that shit. Y'all both crazy 'bout each other. But once the trust has been broken can it really be fixed?" Doc asked. He liked Bonnie, but no woman was worth the trouble Bonnie had put Biz through and if he was willing to touch fire dealing with her, he just wanted his friend to be careful. He rose out his seat and gave Biz a brotherly hug before walking out the door. Biz knew Doc was right, and he had been using much restraint while dealing with Bonnie. He couldn't afford to slip up again. He couldn't afford to be buried because he was blinded by her. They had to be able to co-exist and maybe that was all that they were going to be able to do.

He headed up the stairs and knocked on the door to the room she stayed in before pushing it open. She sat at her vanity brushing her tresses, no makeup, no lashes, eyebrows undone, but to him she was breathtaking. She turned her chair around facing him, displaying her slight attitude. "You know you can't control my body, right? Yes, we may be having a baby, but that controlling shit is dead. I'm not a little ass girl, I'm not going nowhere, and this baby isn't only yours."

Biz nodded his head and walked towards her standing over her, letting her rant. It was the hormones. She didn't realize but her hormones had her emotions all over the place. He didn't argue, he just stared before kneeling down onto his knees and staring at her stomach. "Can I touch you?"

Bonnie was taken by surprise and the thought of his hands on her excited her. She nodded her head, knowing that if she said the words it would probably change his mind. He placed his hand on her small bulge and rubbed. Bonnie just wished that the moment would last forever. He looked up at her and she ran her hand through his scalp and rubbed. Just something as simple as a rub spoke volumes to the two of them. She put her forehead to his wanting to just jump the gun and kiss him, but she knew that if he rejected her that she wouldn't appreciate it. What she didn't know was Biz couldn't reject her if he wanted to. She had opened up a beast in him and that beast loved everything about her. His rubs turned into caresses as his hands began to go farther up brushing underneath her breast. *Fuck it,* Bonnie thought as she leaned in and put her lips into his. He parted his lips inviting her tongue in and she kissed him like it would be her last. He pulled away putting his head down, knowing exactly what he was getting himself into but willing to take all kind of risks when it came to this queen. He stood up swooping her out the chair and carried her to the bed laying her down softly. He looked at her in the eyes and she stared back. He used his hand to brush her hair off her face and just admire her. "I love you," she said, and he knew he couldn't say it back. There was a line that he couldn't cross with Bonnie and he was standing on it. He leaned in and kissed her lips before getting off the bed and walking out the room.

Bonnie hopped up off the bed and walked out after him, grabbing his arm and spinning him around to face her. She wanted answers and she was going to get them. "Why don't you want me?!" Biz just looked on at her knowing that his rejection had bruised her ego, and that wasn't what he was trying to do. "I know you know I want you! So, what's up with these mind games? This ain't the Biz I know."

She was right. Biz had always been open with her before and it was a mistake that he had made getting comfortable and a mistake he couldn't afford to take again. "The Biz you know is dead ma," he said while pointing at his chest and his face, letting her know that she had killed him once and he wouldn't allow her a second chance to do that. Those words to Bonnie were like daggers to her heart. She had fucked up bad and she was trying to think of every way to fix it but somehow, she was always coming up short. She decided she would get off the topic of him accepting her because she couldn't take anything else he would possibly tell her regarding what they were.

"I need my hair done," she said with tight lips, not trying to show any emotion. Biz saw right through her. He knew that his words cut her deep. He knew her better than she knew herself, but he let her believe that he was oblivious to her and how she felt.

"I'll make a phone call," he said before turning and walking away into his bedroom. Bonnie was high maintenance when it came to pampering herself and he couldn't take that from her. It was one of the things that made him gravitate towards her, second to her being able to kill as well as he did. He knew he would have to loosen up one day, that day just wasn't today.

15

SPARKS FLYING

"You stuck around even when the world frowned on me. Kicked me when I was down, and so they clowned on me. Down for me, my homie."

— J. COLE

*H*arper began packing the last of her and CJ's things. Today was the day that they were finally going to be in their own space. After giving her realtor the paperwork, she had to wait two weeks for the slight renovations before moving in. She had told CJ but his mind couldn't register what was going on. He was constantly asking questions about why they were moving, where they were moving, where was his dad. She redirected every question as if she were dodging a bullet. She knew it would only work for some time. But she didn't mind that; she took the time to think of different ways that she could tell CJ the truth. But how did you really tell a 6-year-old that the father they knew all their life wasn't their dad? Scratch that. How did you tell him that the man he had grown up knowing as his father was dead? Harper wanted to avoid telling CJ the truth as much as she could. She wasn't ready to tell the truth about Chris just yet. "Can we go get ice cream before we move into our new house?" CJ asked as he laid on the bed upside down. His mother had packed up his game and there was nothing appealing for him to watch on TV. So laying upside down making funny movements with his feet it was.

"Yes CJ, we can. Now can you please ask Uncle Rara to grab one of these bags?"

"I can do it, I can do it Mommy!" CJ insisted as he hopped off the bed and used all his strength to try and lift up a bag that was just about the same size as he was. Harper looked on and chuckled watching him struggling. "What's in this bag? Weights!?" he asked while pouting his face. His sarcasm made Harper chuckle to herself. CJ was indeed growing into his skin color and there was no point in hiding it anymore. She just wished that Bonnie was around to confide in. Bonnie was nowhere to be found in the past two months and although Havoc seemed to believe that he knew she was alright, Harper couldn't help but to wonder if she really was okay or if she was lying in a ditch somewhere. She didn't press the situation to him too much; she had taken his word and left it at that.

"I heard my name, wassup?" Havoc said interrupting Harper's thoughts and watching CJ still struggle trying to carry the bag.

"Whew. Thank goodness you came up here. Mommy needs help with this bag and my muscles aren't working right now. So, yea," CJ convinced him.

Havoc chuckled while raising an eyebrow to CJ then looking at Harper whose face turned blush. That seemed to be happening a lot for the two of them, the chuckling and the blushing. Ever since Harper had killed Chris, Havoc had felt like he owed her the same loyalty she showed him and Bonnie. They spent more time together, and there was definitely some flirting in the air. Havoc was spending majority of his time with Harper and CJ and he was sending Ivory on killing sprees. "Aight lil' man, I got this. Just let me know when your muscles start working again."

"Well, Mommy and I are going to get some ice cream, my muscles should be working then so I think you need to be around when they do so I could show you how strong I am," CJ boasted while flexing his small arms.

Harper and Havoc both let out a small laugh. Havoc looked to Harper on approval of tagging along and she just shrugged her shoulders acting as if she didn't really care, when in reality her stomach was all bubbly. She had developed a slight crush on Havoc while living with him and even though the way he was living wasn't for her, good girls always fell for bad boys and to her, that's what Havoc was. He wasn't scared of a single thing, and he was all muscle inside and out. She had taken him for arrogant before but realized that arrogance was Havoc. "Aight man, your muscles better start working after that ice cream 'cause ice cream makes my muscles stop working."

"DEAL!" CJ exclaimed, stepping back from the bag and letting Havoc pick it up. He followed Havoc out the room and to the car. Havoc had become a big deal to CJ's life in the short time that they had been living with him. And Harper knew that CJ would miss him. What she didn't know was that Havoc would miss CJ too. Havoc was hard in every sense of the word, but with kids held his soft spot. His own childhood taken from him, he didn't want any kid to suffer the pain he suffered, and that was why he had taken Ivory under the wing and didn't mind playing video games with CJ. Every young boy needed a father and Havoc believed that.

Harper rose off the floor picking up the second bag with her belongings in it and headed out the house meeting CJ and Havoc at her car. She put her bag in the trunk and drove off. She let some music play softly as CJ talked on and on about some kids at his school. After about fifteen minutes, there they were at the ice cream shop. She got out the car and opened the door for CJ as he began sprinting into the store.

"Thank you for everything again," Harper said. She had thanked him a million times and still didn't think it was enough.

"I told you it was cool Harper, stop thanking a nigga. You straight. You did me a solid, showing me how thankful you were. Let's move past it."

Harper nodded her head as they stepped into the ice cream shop and CJ was already at the register ordering. "I want a waffle cone with one scoop of chocolate, one scoop vanilla, with sprinkles, gummy bears and fudge."

Harper just shook her head. Knowing her son, his eyes were bigger than his belly and there was no way he was going to finish that. "I'll take a vanilla cone with sprinkles," she said keeping it simple and stepping aside so Havoc could order.

"Let me get a strawberry banana smoothie." Harper and CJ both looked at him like he had grown two heads. Here they were in an ice cream shop and this man was ordering a smoothie. She shook her head as he dug in his pocket handing the lady a twenty-dollar bill." Keep the change."

"A smoothie? I'm convinced you're scared of sugar," Harper joked, and Havoc chuckled. He kept his sugar eating to the bare minimum. A message came through to his phone and the minute he opened the message the slight smile on his face completely dropped. A picture of him, Harper, and CJ in the ice cream shop let him know that someone was watching him. He looked out the big glass window of the ice cream shop to see if he would spot anyone that he knew. Harper picked up on his demeanor change but didn't say a word. They got their treats and sat at a table.

Havoc was in his own world staring out the glass window being aware of his surroundings. CJ wouldn't stop talking about how good his ice cream was. Havoc didn't want to alarm them, but Harper was no dummy. The seriousness on Havoc's face let her know that something was wrong and that was all that she knew. She didn't know if she was allowed to ask. And wasn't trying to overstep. She could tell Havoc was ready to get up out of there and so she began to scarf down her ice cream. CJ paid attention to her and began to mentally race her and see who could finish first.

After her and CJ finished eating they left out the ice cream shop. "I'll drive," Havoc insisted. Harper didn't reject him; she passed him the car keys. He hopped in the driver side and she got in the passenger and he drove off to the address of her new place. He had made unnecessary turns making sure that no one was following him. Paranoia had definitely set. After pulling up to her house, he let her and CJ get out before asking her of another favor. "Can I use your car? I'll bring it back in one piece." Harper just nodded her head. She owed him her life and she would give him whatever it was that he asked for. He watched as she and CJ got into the house before driving off. He pulled out his phone again looking at the picture and the angle it was taken. The picture had been taken from a side angle and as he began to think of who could have been watching him, he thought of Bonnie. *Maybe she was in trouble*, he thought. His mind was unclear at the moment; every time he thought of who could be coming after him his mind went blank. He didn't like mind games and he wasn't about to play them. He drove to his house and went around loading all his guns that he kept around the house. Whoever wanted smoke was gonna get some and he wouldn't back down from a fight. He thought about calling Ivory over but thought against it. They wanted him and he wasn't going out without a fight.

After loading up all the guns around his house, he grabbed his AK sitting it on his lap before sitting back waiting. He didn't know what exactly he was waiting on but he was blasting whoever and whatever.

16

THE UGLY TRUTH

"There are no secrets that time does not reveal."

— JEAN RACINE

Bonnie sat in front of her laptop with a bowl of Trix cereal as she completed one of her many school assignments. She had enrolled herself in online classes at Yale university to occupy her time whenever she wasn't working. Harper had inspired her seeing as though she never had any time, she was always at her internship program. Bonnie had registered in school because she was bored and never really thought she'd finish it out. But she had surprised herself. This was her last semester before she would officially be a Yale graduate. A young girl from the streets with no parents, a Yale graduate? It almost scared her but made her prouder of herself. This was the most normalcy that she could get, and she knew it. She didn't even have the courage to be able to attend an actual class because she couldn't afford ever being spotted. While Havoc had gotten lucky and made a best friend, the rest of their coworkers, especially the females, hated Bonnie. She was bringing in the most money, with the most efficient kills. Although she was the youngest, she was one of the best and they hated it. But Bonnie didn't give a rat's ass. A lot of them didn't understand that she was doing this because it was the only thing she was good at. She was a devil in a red dress, her commanding presence was what made heads turn, and it was nothing she could or would do about it.

"Babe, how long before you done with that long ass essay? I need some ass," Khalil shouted from the bedroom. Bonnie chuckled to herself while shaking her head. Khalil was the only man that she had let her guards down for. She didn't play when it came to her heart because she couldn't see herself going through heartbreak like people on TV. She wasn't levelheaded enough to deal with the liars and the cheaters and everything else that came with men and their games. But Khalil had shown her that he wasn't with none of that. After making him chase her for about three years, she finally let him in and he did everything different from what she'd seen on TV. He was her McDreamy and she was his Meredith Grey. They were inseparable and no matter what, the love they had was undeniable. She went over her essay one last time before submitting it to her professor and closed her laptop. Twenty thousand words on Ted Bundy and how he got away with what he did was now submitted. Bonnie's interest in criminology put her two steps ahead of the game when it came to her real life and she used everything she learned and applied it to herself. Another reason that she wouldn't ever get caught up.

She rose out her seat and walked into the bedroom and she was taken away at what she saw. There were candles lit all around and flower petals all over the bed. With her jaw touching her chest, Khalil walked over closing her mouth. "We don't want any flies to get in there," he joked, and Bonnie laughed, swatting his hand away.

"Aww, this is so nice! Look at you being all mushy,." Bonnie teased as she walked over to the bed where there were chocolate covered strawberries.

Khalil shrugged his shoulder, not caring about his masculinity when it came to Bonnie. That was his woman and he would do anything to make her feel special. "You know your man be trying. I got all this girly shit going on. YouTube helped a nigga out," he replied while grabbing the chocolate syrup he'd brought into the room and began massaging her feet. Bonnie laid back and let him do his thing. He massaged her foot and used his tongue to suck each and every one of her toes. To him, she had the sweetest skin he'd ever tasted.

"Mmm," Bonnie said, letting out a small moan. Khalil's foreplay was better than his actual pipe game, but she wasn't complaining. He got the job done each and every time. She threw her head back as he put a little syrup on her inner thigh and licked it all up, caressing her skin with his tongue. With her eyes closed, she let him massage her body. It was well needed. She had been out every day this week putting someone to rest and the one day she had to herself was dedicated to her school work. She appreciated Khalil and didn't know what she would do without him.

After a few seconds of Khalil not feeling on her body, she sat up and her mouth dropped to her chest again. Khalil was on one knee with a princess-cut diamond ring. She couldn't believe it and needed to hear him say it. Her life was no fairytale. Marriage was nothing but a dream to her, but here Khalil was making it her reality.

"I know we ain't been together for nothing more of seven months, but a nigga knew from day one that he wanted your fine ass. Now that a nigga got you, I ain't tryna let you go ma. A nigga playing for keeps. Imma ask you this corny ass question and you better say yes or imma beat cho ass. Will you marry me?" he asked flashing a smile.

Bonnie couldn't help but to laugh. What a proposal. Khalil always showed her a different side of him from what everyone else saw. She nodded her head and jumped on him. "Yes!"

He smiled at her reaction and slid the ring on her finger before kissing her. "I love you ma."

"I love you too Khalil."

Bonnie's eyes opened and standing over her was Biz with a grill on his face. She didn't know if she had been talking in her sleep or smiling too hard for his liking, but whatever it was made her chuckle because he was showcasing some kind of jealousy.

Lately she had been dreaming about Khalil and she felt like it was a sign. She didn't feel like he would rest in perfect peace until the person who put the hit out on him was laid to rest. And she was going to make sure of it. She didn't know where exactly she would start, but she was in the lion's den. If she had any chance of finding out about the hit, she was at the perfect place. "I'm going for a run."

Bonnie sat up and looked at the clock and it was pushing 3:00 p.m. Biz had finally gotten out the house, and although he was laying low he put a daily workout into his plan. Bonnie wanted to go with him but she dared not ask. She had been rejected by him enough and she knew the answer flat out already. "Can you grab me gushers, popcorn and fruit rollups while you're out?" she asked as she followed him out the room.

"Ask Khalil," he mumbled under his breath, not knowing that she heard him. A smile spread across her face as she grabbed his arm and turned him to face her.

"Ooh, baby, green looks good on your fine ass," she joked, making the corner of Biz's lips turn to a slight curve. He turned away and walked out letting her lock the door with no other words. Bonnie couldn't believe that she had Biz jealous. He had shown her that he didn't care and that they would never be time and time again, but this jealousy gave her hope again.

She walked from the door and took a seat on the couch thinking about where Biz would keep anything important. She needed to snoop around and she had to fast. The only way to find out where Biz had held all of Dead Silence's paperwork was to become Biz. She had to turn her mind into his own. He was organized and private, so everything would all be hidden in one place. She walked up the stairs as if she was going to the bedroom and stopped in her tracks. Nah, he wouldn't put it there. He's more of a garage or basement kind of guy.

She walked to the garage that had previously been her hostage spot and all the mess that was once there was no longer there. She looked around and nothing; it was just an empty garage. She turned on her heels walking back into the house and began to think. There was no basement to the house so that was out of the question.

After sitting for about thirty minutes trying to collect her thoughts, it was as if a lightbulb had went off in her head. The attic. She ran up the stairs and passed the bedrooms and went up the second flight of stairs. The door was surprisingly unlocked and she took that as her moment of opportunity. She ran up the stairs and what she saw was just what she had expected. There were file cabinets and his unfinished plans for Havoc with pictures of Harper, Ivory, Havoc, and CJ on the wall.

Confusion took over Bonnie as she thought about what Harper and CJ had to do with anything, and she would definitely bring it to Biz's attention that she had nothing to do with anything. For the first time, she wanted to know what was going on in the outside world. A picture of

Harper, Havoc and CJ getting ice cream confused her. What was Havoc doing with Harper? Was he trying to kill her? A million questions went on in her mind and she had to store them in her mental, keeping her mind on the prize.

She walked to the file cabinet and began to snatch them open. There was a folder for every assassin down with the organization. She pulled out her own folder and inside was her picture with a star beside it, the number of kills, the name of each kill, who had ordered the kills, and the account numbers that the money had been wire transferred from. Biz had kept all this information because if he was to ever go down, so was half of the politicians that had put him to the job. He was smart and just kept this information where no one else had access to it. Until today, no one else had known of these files. She shoved her file back and looked at the clock, knowing that he would be back in any minute, but she wasn't leaving without an answer. She knew this was the closest she would get to the truth and wouldn't leave without it.

She pulled out Khalil's file and he too had a star beside his picture with the word deceased. *What the fuck were these stars?* she began to think to herself. She would ask Biz the minute she saw him. She went through Khalil's folder flipping to the last page. Her palms began to sweat as she scanned the paper. The five-million-dollar wire transfer made Bonnie's brows arch. Who would want Khalil dead that bad? She continued to scan and the minute her eyes fell onto the name of the person who put out the hit, she could feel Biz standing in the doorway.

"You found what you was looking for?" Everything in Bonnie wanted her to cry out in this moment, but the shock that consumed her wouldn't let her. She turned to Biz with distraught obvious on her face.

"You knew?" she asked with a shaky voice, and he nodded his head before taking a few steps towards her. He knew she was about to explode whether it be with tears or with anger, and he wanted to be sure to console her. She felt how he felt the day she had betrayed him. Because now the shoe was on the other foot. She was the one betrayed by the only other person in the world that she trusted. "She wouldn't!" Bonnie defended, not wanting to believe what her eyes had seen, but her eyes weren't deceiving her; her best friend was.

17

DREAMS AND NIGHTMARES

"My best dreams and worst nightmares have the same people in them."

— PHILIPPOS

*H*arper sat in the park with CJ letting him run around and play basketball trying to burn all the energy of his that she could. Even after leaving his after school program he still had energy to burn. She had been working a lot lately and being a single mom had her drained. She silently saluted and tipped her hat to every women who had managed to do it before her. She had come from work picking him up from practice and straight to the park with her scrubs on. She had enrolled him in all kind of extracurricular activities to occupy his time so he wouldn't have any questions, and it worked. Between the basketball team, swim classes, and karate, he was drained and all that he was able to do was eat and sleep, but today was different. She didn't know if they didn't do their usual activities but CJ had so much energy to burn and she didn't, so the only way to help him was to take him to the park.

It had been four weeks since leaving Havoc's home and Harper hadn't spoken to him since. The last time she had seen him he'd been acting strange, and he had Ivory drop her car back off to her. She wanted to call and check up on him, but she wasn't sure if that was her place. She didn't really know where they stood, and didn't want to make things weird. She didn't know if what she felt for Havoc was real and whether the feeling was mutual. She had summed it up to her just being in the presence of a powerful man. This was the most that her and Havoc had interacted, and it was all because of Bonnie's disappearance. Bonnie was another one weighing heavily on her mind. All hopes that her friend was alive had finally went away. It wasn't like Bonnie to go MIA. Although Havoc seemed confident that she was alive, Harper wasn't the least bit convinced. She looked over at CJ who was playing with some other kids around his age and smiled. That smile on her baby boy's face was all that she ever wanted. She let out a small yawn and felt her eyelids begin to get heavy. After a twelve-hour shift, mommy duties were definitely kicking her ass, but what could she do. Being a mom wasn't a part-time job. Being a mom was like being married to a kid, in sickness and health, for better or worse, no matter the circumstances. Being a mother was taking vows and although it was exhausting, Harper wouldn't trade it for the world. Her eyes began to close on their own and she let them. As long as she could hear that silly little laugh, she knew CJ was alright.

"Ahhh Mommy!!!" CJ yelled as he kicked and screamed causing people in the park to look on as he got carried over someone's shoulder.

Harper's eyes shot open frantically as she looked around the playground. Parents were all looking around for who the young boy's parent was. Harper didn't know how long she had closed her eyes for, but a mother's worst nightmare was happening.

When she finally laid eyes on CJ, he was being thrown in the back of a van. Harper took off running towards it leaving all her belongings behind and knowing in her mind that she didn't stand a chance. But that didn't stop her from running until the van peeled off burning rubber.

She looked around the playground feeling like a woman off an abduction movie as all the people nearby stared on in shock and held their kids close to them. Her heart was beating out of her chest and the panic that had set in wouldn't allow her to think straight. She thought about jumping in her car and chasing the van, but it was no use seeing as though she had left all her belongings on the bench. She watched as the car got farther and farther away and with the more distance, her heart broke into smaller pieces. She ran back to the bench where her things were and grabbed her phone and keys. She had managed on being independent but when it came to situations like this, she couldn't. She dialed the one person who had been there time and time again for her and just hoped that he answered. "Yo?"

"They took CJ!!" she yelled, not able to get anything else out as the tears began to pour from her soul.

"Who? Where are you?" Havoc asked. The panic in his voice made her ease up a little, letting her know that she wasn't alone. It wasn't just her that cared about CJ's well being, Havoc did too. Even though he didn't express it, the tone in his voice said otherwise.

Harper tried pulling herself together as she saw bystanders all on the phone and heard police sirens in the distance. If she didn't have Havoc on her side, she surely would have waited for the police to show up and used their help. But since Havoc was on her side, she no longer needed the police. Her faith was in Havoc and she held him at a pedestal higher than the police ever could. With the police, she knew after forty-eight hours they would believe that CJ was dead and would put his case on the back burner, but with Havoc, CJ was the number one priority and that was the support that she needed. She didn't know how exactly Havoc would find him, but she put her trust in him.

"I'm on my way," she said while jumping into her car and speeding off before the police came.

* * *

"WHAT COLOR WAS THE CAR? What did the niggas look like?" Havoc asked the minute he opened the door. Harper's eyes were bloodshot red from the lack of sleep and from crying the entire drive. Havoc wanted answers but he could visibly see that in her state of mind, she would be no good giving out information. She fell into his chest and just began to bawl out in tears. Havoc just let her cry in his chest, standing there awkwardly. He knew she needed to get it out, but time was something they didn't have.

It was as if Harper could read his mind because she pulled back and wiped her face off and walked into the house. Ivory was sitting on the couch ready to shoot any and everything in his way. All he needed was the name and the face and he was handling it. He could see the distress all over Harper's face and wanted to do nothing more than to help. In the time that she had spent in Havoc's house, Harper had helped him out and it didn't go unnoticed. From checking on his skin brand to leaving him food on the counter with his name on it, he appreciated all the gestures. Harper took a seat beside him and Havoc sat across from her waiting to hear her speak.

"I fell asleep. I fell asleep at the fucking playground!" she said, getting upset with herself. She felt like had she never closed her eyes, she would have her son. But she had no idea that whether she was standing right beside CJ or a hop, skip and a jump away, the people who had him were on a mission and it was best that she wasn't in their way.

"Did you see anything?" Havoc asked, hoping for a clue. Knowing that without any information everything would be much harder.

"No, I just heard CJ call out for me," she said with tears beginning to fall from her eyes again. The fear of never seeing her son again was eating at her. The sound of his voice calling out for her made her feel like the worst mom on the planet. She just wanted to rewind the hands of time and take CJ home the minute she felt like sleep was consuming her. But there was nothing she could do.

"Go rest. I'll make some phone calls. Ivy, go to the playground and see what people talking about. See if anyone seen or heard anything." He nodded his head before walking out the door. Harper wanted to decline his offer of going to bed, but she knew that right now sleep was well needed. She rose up off the couch and went into the bedroom that she and CJ used to share. She just hoped that her son was alright, and that whoever had him didn't harm him.

Havoc took a seat on the couch with a million thoughts on his mind. Something in him knew that whoever had CJ was fucking with him. He had heard nothing since receiving the picture at the ice cream shop, but he knew shit wasn't sweet. He had his guards up but never thought that Harper and CJ would get caught in the crossfire. He wasn't going to tell Harper anything until he was one hundred percent sure.

He turned to the news and just as he thought, the abduction was written all over the headlines, but nobody knew a single thing. There was a sketch of Harper and the authorities were looking for her for questioning. There were bystanders standing all around gossiping and Havoc just hoped that Ivory was able to talk to one of them. The rules of the streets were no snitching, but how many people really did go by that? Not a bunch of parents who had witnessed a kidnapping. The thought of that could have been any one of their children alone made them sing like canaries. About an hour later, Ivory was back at the house and taking a seat with Havoc. "What's the word?" Havoc asked.

"A black van with tinted out windows, so no one could see who the driver was, and a man about your height snatched him up."

Havoc's mind continued to go blank and nothing was coming up. He picked up his phone and realized he had gotten a picture message. When he opened it up, not to much surprise, there was a picture of CJ's hands and feet tied up to a chair. CJ looked as if he was trying to break free but his little six-year-old body couldn't. The message below the picture said "Rest in Peace." Havoc tossed the phone down. He knew that whoever had CJ was trying to get to him. He couldn't live with the fact of something happening to a child because of him. He had killed hundreds of people but children were off limits to him. It seemed like the karma of every kill he had done was coming back to him and in the worst way. He picked up the phone trying to examine the picture and see if he realized anything familiar that could tell him where CJ was, but nothing. He couldn't tell Harper of the message that he had received. Because he wouldn't allow for anything to happen to CJ.

Havoc: **Name your price.**

He texted back to the unknown number. He was on a time crunch. Had it been any other kid, he wouldn't feel bad about their death being on his hands, but CJ was different. They had bonded and formed their own type of relationship. Letting his death be on his hands would change Havoc forever, and he knew it. He waited for a reply from the number and nothing came. It was almost as if he was playing a waiting game.

18

LOVE VS. DECEIT

"Love is many things, but it is never deceitful. Nothing toxic comes from genuine love."

— UNKNOWN

*H*avoc and Bonnie both sat on the bed with completely different thoughts rummaging through their heads. Her mind couldn't register what she had found out about Khalil's hit. There had to be some kind of error somewhere down the line, because Harper? Harper of all people put a hit out on Khalil? She never understood when people would say the truth hurts, but here she was living and hurting because of the truth. She couldn't wrap her head around it and wanted to be in denial about it. But with the way Biz had everything set up in those file cabinets, it was so organized that a fine tooth comb could go through it and there would be no error.

When the realization that it was the truth had somewhat settled in her, she began to think what would make Harper put a five-million-dollar hit on Khalil. What did he do to her that was that bad? She knew all her assumptions and thoughts would continue to come up blank until she heard it from the horse's mouth. "Are you sure?" Bonnie asked for what seemed like the millionth time in a matter of weeks, and Biz was about tired of the same question. He had seen someone in shock but the type of shock that Bonnie was displaying was different. He didn't know if it was the pregnancy or if it was just her initial reaction being that she had a relationship with the person who put out the hit and the person who was killed but whatever it was, he needed her to get over it. They had bigger fish to fry.

"For the last time, yes. And don't ask me again. Now you know how it feels to be betrayed by someone you trusted with your life."

Shots fired, Bonnie thought to herself. If this was what Biz felt like when she had turned on him, then she was tremendously sorry. This kind of hurt only came when you loved someone and although Biz hadn't said it, Bonnie knew it. The love that she thought was there that he kept trying to downplay wasn't a figment of her imagination; it was her reality. But that wasn't her focus right now.

Biz stared at the burner phone in his hand. He had kidnapped CJ and he knew that children were Havoc's weakness. He knew Havoc like the back of his hand and knew well enough that this kidnapping would trigger him. He had taken CJ with the thought of killing him but the father figure in him that was growing daily tried talking him out of it. CJ was just a kid that had gotten caught in the crossfire. He was paying for Havoc's sin and even though it wasn't right, Biz had a point to prove. He couldn't be fucked with, he wouldn't be fucked with. This was a lesson to Havoc and to whoever else that had ever planned on crossing him, Bonnie included. He didn't want to put an innocent kid to rest but he felt like he had no choice. It had been three days since Havoc had sent a text, and Biz still hadn't replied. Anticipation was a bitch, and he knew Havoc was probably losing his mind because he had no control over this situation.

He rose off the bed and began to walk out the bedroom with Bonnie on his tail. She had seen that Biz had taken CJ and she knew exactly what was in store for him. But the hate in her heart that she felt for Harper wouldn't allow her to feel sorry for her son. She had killed children before and not an ounce of guilt had ever consumed her. This wouldn't be the first innocent child's death that she witnessed, but the motherly instinct in her caused her to speak up. Not because Harper was her friend; with the way that she felt now, Harper was her enemy. But her motherly instincts and the constant kicking of her baby reminded her that one day that could be her own child in the situation. CJ had done nothing wrong to deserve his fate. But his mother and Havoc had done enough to make someone want to put a bullet through him. She wanted to hate CJ and call it even with Harper after putting her son to rest, but the wild kicks in her belly were a sign from her baby to stop in her tracks.

Just as he reached the garage door, Bonnie managed to speak up. "Cripple him." Biz turned to her trying to understand what exactly she meant by that and knowing that she had his attention, she continued. "Havoc, killing CJ will hurt him, but in the end, we still walk away with nothing. I know you got a stash but how long can we really live off of it? If he killed everyone with Dead Silence, that means he's carrying out kills alone, meaning that he's making bank. Put a dent in his pocket in exchange for CJ." Biz thought about what Bonnie was saying and it wasn't a bad idea at all. Get the money, do the exchange and of course, Havoc wouldn't walk away alive. So by the end of the transaction, he would be circled in chalk. So, he was going to have his cake and eat it too. Bonnie had no idea that her quick thinking was what made her such a great assassin. In fact, she was the best assassin he'd ever had. She didn't know it, but that shit turned him on as well.

"That's perfect," he replied. Her plan was the best plan and although he didn't want to show her his excitement, he pulled her in and kissed her on the forehead. Bonnie just walked away. She had noticed that the more she threw herself on Biz the more he rejected her, but as soon as she fell back, he was on her body like a tattoo.

"Tell him you want a hundred mil, all in hundreds," Bonnie said as she entered the kitchen to make CJ something to eat. Biz had raised his brows at her as he walked behind her. He was thinking more of fifty mil, but a hundred million definitely sounded much better. Being out of that much money would sure enough put a dent in what Havoc though he was controlling but it would be just enough for Biz to be back on top and take over the business he started even though he didn't have to.

The only reason why he wanted the business back at this point was because Bonnie was having his child and he wanted to have something to pass down to it. Dead Silence had been his baby before but now that he was actually having a baby, it was time for him to make Dead Silence the biggest international kill for hire organization that was out.

Biz: **ONE HUNDRED MILLION ALL HUNDREDS, FRIDAY. LOCATION:TBD**

"You want a sandwich?" Bonnie asked as she began to put one together for her and CJ. Biz shrugged his shoulders and she took that for a yes. "When is the drop off date?" she asked curiously.

"In four days."

"I'm coming. I need answers and she is the only person I can get them from. Being that it's her son, she is predictable, and I know that Havoc will have her there for the exchange."

Biz shook his head. "Nah, I can't risk something happening to you. You know your brother better than anyone. The nigga is a hot head. You carrying my seed and I need you to stay here."

"I haven't defied you yet, I've proven my loyalty to you. This isn't something that I'm sweeping under the rug. I need to see her because I need to hear it from her mouth that she ordered Khalil's kill and I need her to give me a good enough reason for why I still shouldn't kill her son after we get that money," Bonnie replied, letting Biz know that she wasn't asking she was telling him that she would be there. Biz knew there was no debating with her; right now he knew there was nothing he could say that would make her change her mind.

"Aight B, you got it. If anything, use that lil' nigga as a shield."

"I won't have to," she replied and cut all three sandwiches down the middle before giving him one. "Since he will be here for four more days, he'll be taking over the damn dungeon room you kept me in and I'll be sleeping in the master suite. You can pick where you wanna sleep but again, its non-debatable. He needs clothes by the way."

Biz just took a bite into his sandwich watching as Bonnie took CJ his food. He knew that he couldn't control himself to even be in the same room as her, so sharing a bed was out of the question. He hurried up finishing the sandwich before going out to get CJ clothes. Bonnie had shown him loyalty with the plan that she had come up with and he wanted to just move forward from what had transpired between the two of them, but it was almost impossible. Every time he looked in the mirror he was reminded why he shouldn't trust a soul.

Bonnie had untied CJ, revealing herself to him for the first time since he had been there, and the look of a familiar face caused him to pounce on her. "Aww, Auntie B, you don't understand how happy I am to see you. I was so scared," he said before pulling her in for a hug. Although she was telling herself to hate the woman who had created him, his innocence was warming her heart. She hated that he was in the predicament that he was in, and under any other circumstance she would've told Biz to give him back to his mother. But she couldn't; she needed to see Harper and the only way was through CJ. Yes, he was being used as a pawn but he was better as a pawn, than he was a corpse.

"Here baby, I made you a sandwich," she said pulling away from him and letting him have a seat on the cold cement ground beside her. He was so much more comfortable being that Bonnie was there with him. He had been locked in the same garage that Bonnie had once been tied up in and she knew that he was ready to get some good ole rest in an actual bed. She watched as he scarfed down the sandwich as if he hadn't eaten in days, but she knew that was a factor in his greediness because every day that he had been there she had personally made his food each and every time with the thought of even possibly poisoning him.

"Are you ready to shower and get ready for bed?" she asked, trying to make light of his situation, and he just shook his head.

"I want my mommy," he said with tear-filled eyes. She could see that he was drained and that his little six-year-old brain had no idea what was going on.

"Your mommy is busy, Chris. Maybe after you shower and get ready for bed we can probably call her," she swindled. He nodded his head before standing to his feet and grabbing her hand as they went back into the house and into the room that Bonnie slept in. She ran him a bath, using her body wash to make bubbles for him, and watched as he played alone.

Although she was six and a half months pregnant, the reality of actually having a baby to care and nurture for hadn't hit her yet She knew it wouldn't be long before she had to retire from the game; she couldn't afford to put her child's life in jeopardy. Murder for hire was a man's game and she just happened to be really good at it, but she knew it wouldn't be long before she would meet her maker if she continued. She had already slipped up and gotten kidnapped by Biz. There wasn't no telling who else was out there that wished that they had gotten the same opportunity that Biz had. After watching CJ blow bubbles and begin to yawn, she rinsed him off then dressed him up in the clothes that Biz had brought for him. Although he was only staying for four days, Biz had bought enough clothes for four weeks; not knowing what size he wore, he just grabbed a whole rack of clothing.

Bonnie finally laid CJ in the bed and headed for the door. "Aunt B, you said we'd call my mommy."

"CJ, she is sleeping. She told me she would call you after work," Bonnie lied, putting the young boy at ease. He nodded his head yawning one last time before Bonnie walked out and locked him inside the room. The same room she had felt like a prisoner in, she was holding her own captive.

She entered the master bedroom for the first time and although it was big enough to be a studio apartment, it had the least bit inside. A bed, in the middle of the room, and a closet was all that was there. She knew that Biz was organized but she didn't think it was to this extent. She shook her head from side to side, but she wasn't complaining. She preferred a neat, clean room than a messy one. She walked into the connected bathroom and Biz was in a bubble-filled bath with his head tilted back and his eyes closed as instrumentals from Motown Records played serenading him and he hummed along. Bonnie wanted to interrupt him but thought against it as she stripped out her shorts and tank top, walking towards the bath and getting in. She sat across from him and instead of him getting out and walking away, he figured he'd just enjoy himself. He knew Bonnie well enough to know that she wouldn't quit, and he was about tired of the cat and mouse games.

She put her head back and he grabbed one of her feet while massaging it beneath the water. The feeling to Bonnie was euphoric. She wasn't thinking sexual at the moment; she was thinking that her swollen, pregnant foot felt amazing being caressed the way it was. Biz looked at her then at her neatly done toes and kissed each and every one of them. The feeling of his soft lips against her toes alone sent a shock through her pussy. She wanted to pull away but wouldn't dare because she knew that once she pulled away, she wouldn't be guaranteed this moment again. She let out a small moan and Biz let out a smile. Although he knew playing with

Bonnie was like playing with fire, he took the chance anyway. He scooted closer to her and pulled her legs around him causing her to be sitting directly on his wood and facing him. She looked into his eyes with hope that he would fuck her senseless right here in the bath, but he pulled her in for a kiss, sucking and tugging at her tongue and lips. She grabbed his dick and put it at the entrance of her womanhood; one stroke in and she was gasping for air. He wanted to finish what they had started but he knew that right now wasn't the time to complicated things. He used his hips to thrust in her one more time as he clenched his jaw at how tight she was and pulled out. Bonnie's eyes shot open as if he had lost his mind. She needed this and he was playing with her emotions. She had no idea how badly he wanted it, but instead of continuing what they had started, he stood up from the bath about to get out but she wasn't giving up that easily. She needed to get her nut off and if she needed to do it herself she would, but she was going to do it her way. She wrapped her lips around his dick and bobbed her head up and down letting it touch the back of her throat. While she used her hand to finger herself, Biz grabbed the back of her head and it made her go even crazier. She knew exactly how he liked it and was going to show him what he was missing out on. It wasn't long before he came, and she swallowed every drop while releasing her own cum. She looked up at him with an innocence in her eyes, but he knew she was far from that. He stepped into the shower and washed off quickly just as Bonnie had made her entrance in. He knew that he had slipped up a little more than he would have liked, but patted himself on the back for not going all the way through with her. Bonnie made a nigga's mental get cloudy and foggy. The pussy was that good and right now, he needed to be on his A game. He was done playing games with her and with the way she made him feel. When all this was over he was gonna pursue her. He didn't know how it would work, but they had to. She had a nigga fucked up and playing these games with her didn't help. He figured he would know where her loyalty lied at the exchange. That moment would determine where they would go from there. If she stood by him and had his back, then she would be his ride or die bitch. But if she went against him, it was sad to say that it would be a blood bath and he would be the only person walking out of it.

19

LOSSES

"Death is not the greatest loss in life. The greatest loss is what dies inside while still alive."

— NORMAN COUSINS

*H*avoc and Ivory sat at a coffee table with magazines in their hands slightly covering their faces while burning a hole in Braxton Miles' neck. It was funny that one could bark up the wrong tree when money was involved but didn't realize that they couldn't take those dollars with them to the grave. Braxton had no idea what exactly had been coming to him. He was so engaged in his work infiltrating the lives of others that he didn't see how that could cause problems for himself. Chris had hired him to do his dirty work but no amount of money that Chris could have paid him would stop him from reaching his fate. Havoc watched as he snuck pictures of the lady across the coffee shop. He was smooth without a doubt. Anyone would have just thought that he was tapping the frame of his glasses as a thinking method, but he had observed Braxton well enough to know that he didn't wear glasses. It was a part of his disguise and the micro camera that was installed in the frame was capturing pictures of his subject. Havoc nodded to Ivory and rose from the table before walking out the coffee shop. He watched from a distance as Ivory walked past Braxton and purposely dropped a hot cup of coffee on him.

"Oh my god, I'm so sorry!" Ivory said in his kid friendly tone. Braxton just looked up at him and instantly knew who Ivory was. His face went from pale to pink in as quick as two seconds. He had been made and now he was scared for his life. Ivory grabbed a few pieces of tissue off the table and tried helping Braxton get himself cleaned up, but he just declined the offer.

"It's okay, no biggie. I was just heading out anyways." Ivory smirked at Braxton knowing that he was scared for his life, and what could he really do in this coffee shop full of people? Yell out that this young boy killed for a living? He knew just as well as Ivory knew that no one would buy it. He grabbed up his things as Ivory walked to the back restroom. Before he walked out, he looked out the glass window of the coffee shop, paranoid at what Ivory may have had in store for him. He tucked his glasses in his pocket and began rushing down the street once he thought the coast was clear. But Havoc was right on his heel with every step. Braxton was so set on looking ahead he never thought to look back. As he went to cross the street, Ivory pulled up in a minivan directly in front of him. Havoc could already sense the panic as he stuck Braxton with a needle filled with general anesthesia. He lifted Braxton up and put him into the car as Ivory peeled off into the sunset.

"Aghhhh," Braxton yelled as Ivory landed him a punch in the gut, making him crouch over as much as he could because he was tied upside down dangling in the air. Havoc just sat back not saying a word as Ivory landed blow for blow on the white man, bruising him up. After about five minutes, Havoc stood from his seat and walked over to Ivory placing his hand on his shoulder, silently telling him to stop.

"I think Mr. Miles here is ready to talk."

"Yes-yes- yes. Just please let me go. I was just doing my job," Braxton spoke stuttering, showcasing how scared he was for his life.

"Ahhh, doing your job. Why don't you tell me all about it?" Havoc asked. He wanted to know how much Braxton had known about him and who else had known so that everyone could be put in a grave.

"I haven't told anyone, I swear! I have no friends, I'm an only child, my parents are dead, just please let me go," he pleaded.

Havoc began to circle him. He believed Braxton. He was so scared for his life that he would tell nothing but the truth, scared of the repercussions of a lie. "Braxton, we are going to let you go," Havoc said looking at Ivory, who looked at him like he had lost his mind. "But first, I want to know where your flash drive is of all the pictures. I want your phone and computer, then I'll let you go."

"My flash drive and laptop are in the trunk of my car; it's linked to my desktop at home. My phone is in the jacket that I was wearing. You can have it all, just let me go. You will never hear from me again."

Havoc walked over to the jacket that they had taken off of him, already knowing that his phone was in there, he just wanted to see if Braxton would try any funny business when it came to his belongings, but he didn't. "Before I let you go, what all did you find out about me and Ivory?"

"I just witnessed some of your crimes, but I didn't say a word. I swear to God."

"So, the only person you told was Chris?"

Braxton began to nod his head wildly. "He was the only person who paid for the info, so he was the only person who got it."

"Okay, a deal is a deal. I said I'd let you go, so I'm going to let you go," Havoc said while walking over to the table that sat a butcher knife big enough to cut the thick rope and a bucket of water filled to the top. Braxton let out a deep breath, happy to be out of the mess that he was now in. He had never been put in this kind of a position because of his job. But he was thankful that Havoc wasn't as gritty as he had seen him be, or so he thought. Havoc grabbed the bucket of water and put it under Braxton's head. "Goodbye," he said while letting the rope down lower until his head was completely under the water. He sat back watching him squirm until he wasn't anymore, and left his head underneath for good measure.

"I thought you was really gon' let that pale nigga go," Ivory said.

"I did. I never said I was letting him go on his two feet. I let him go meet his maker," Havoc explained then shrugged. He looked through Braxton's phone, reading all the text messages and emails seeing if he had told anybody, and it came up empty.

"Take the van and go scoop up the laptop, computer and flash drive. Imma have someone look through all this shit thoroughly to make sure we ain't slipping," Havoc instructed while leaving the warehouse that had been rented under a false name. He shot the maids a text and the location so they could come clean up behind him. He had been caught slipping when it came to Braxton all because of Chris, but now he was clean, and there was no more time for any more slip-ups.

He jumped in his car and peeled off, heading to his house. The drop was in two days and he had the money. He needed to know that no one was snooping around where they didn't need to be, and he had taken out the two people who had been snooping. He had no idea who had CJ, but this was it. After getting CJ back, he was gonna leave to a different city, leaving Harper and him behind. He had endangered himself and them for simply being there for them and he couldn't afford to endanger himself again. This was why he dealt with women from afar. No one knew how bad giving up a hundred million dollars was denting his pockets, and he wasn't bitching about it. He couldn't remember the last time he had taken a loss that big, and he wasn't ready to take another one any time soon. He wanted to know who had CJ and if shit went how he wanted it to go, he would be leaving with his bread and CJ. But it all depended on how many people showed up at the drop. He wanted to go guns blazing but wouldn't if it was putting his life on the line. He wasn't afraid to die, but if he could avoid it, then why not?

He pulled up to his house and sitting on his couch was Harper with her phone in her hand, hoping, just hoping that a call would come through. "How do we know that he's still alive?" she asked, barely looking up at him. He had watched her transform from full of life to looking like she was a zombie; that's what losing her kid made her look like. She was living like she had no reason to live, like CJ was dead already. Havoc realized that she needed some reassurance and decided to text the unknown number hoping to get an answer.

Havoc: **Proof of life.**

In about two minutes, he received a picture with the current date and time of CJ, who was sitting bored in a chair with a dark background, giving Havoc no way to identify where he was. He turned his phone to Harper and she stared at the picture, seeing that CJ wasn't harmed, and in fact he had on different clothes and whoever it was that had him was actually taking care of him. She was grateful for Havoc because she didn't have as much hope as he had. She jumped up giving him a hug and he let her while wrapping his hands on the small of her back. He knew she needed all the comfort that she could get and although he was bad at giving it, he just wanted her to know that she had him and that he cared just as much about CJ as she did. She looked up at him as he looked down at her. Her hair was all over her face and he pushed it back. Harper leaned in for a kiss and Havoc didn't pull away. He let her devour his mouth as he returned the favor. He couldn't remember the last time he had actually put his lips to another woman's and although it felt so right in the moment, he knew it was so wrong. He pulled away from her taking two steps back.

"I'm no good for you Harp."

"You're good enough. And I am good enough for you. Your bad and my good, make one hell of a combination," she said taking two steps forward towards him, grabbing his hands.

He shook his head as he slid his hands out of her grip. "Nothing good can come from this, look at where CJ's at. That shit is 'cause motherfuckers are after me. I can't risk anything else happening to the two of y'all. Look what Chris did. Made me have to put an innocent nigga in the dirt."

"Once we get CJ back, we'll be more careful. We can relocate. I'm willing to take that chance. CJ looks up to you and if we have to get away from Georgia to be together, then I'm willing to do that with you," Harper explained, closing in the space between the two of them. She wasn't taking no for an answer and Havoc knew it. And somehow, everything she was saying sounded good. On a regular, he wasn't listening to any women trying to push their way into his life. But Harper was different. She was already in his life. She knew what it was from jump, she knew exactly what she was asking to sign up for and if she could accept him flaws and all, who was he to decline? Him thinking about the possibility of them being together made Harper move in closer and wrap her hands around his neck.

Fuck it, he thought as he lifted up her small frame as she wrapped her legs around his waist. Their tongues tangoing with one another, neither one of them wanted to stop. Harper sucked on his bottom lip as he bit on her top. He laid her on the couch and lifted her shirt over her head. He hadn't been intimate with a woman in so long, he had thought he lost his touch. But that was beside the case. All it took was the right woman to bring it out of him, and she was Harper. He kissed on her neck as she arched her back as the tingling sensation ran through her body. She craved the touch of a man. She hadn't been touched by Chris way before she had killed him and the thought alone of that should've been a red flag to her, but it wasn't. The way that Havoc worked on her, it was almost as if their bodies craved one another. He pulled his pants down and watched as she pulled hers down. Her juices were already coated on her lips and ready to take all of him. He kneeled into her while throwing her legs over his shoulders. Just as he was about to enter her, he realized that he didn't have any protection. Harper had picked up on his hesitance almost instantly and directed his eyes to her.

"I'm clean," was all she said and he had taken her word for it as if she had shown him her medical papers. He had come this far and he was ready to feel the inside of her. He slid himself into her and began penetrating her walls as she arched her back and bit her lips. "Ohh, ohh, Havoc!" she yelled as the sensation that filled her took over. She hadn't experienced sex like this ever in her life. With her legs thrown over his shoulders and her hands pinned over her head, she let him take control of her body and she loved every bit of it. "I'm coming!!" she yelled at the top of her voice, and Havoc pulled out of her while flipping her over to her stomach, pulling her ass high in the air as he entered her again. This time his thrusts were harder and faster and before she knew it, she was coming without warning. After witnessing her get off, he pulled out of her and nutted all over her ass. He sat back against the couch as she laid on her stomach falling into slight sleep. They had crossed the line that he had so desperately tried not to, but temptation was a bitch that he never gave in to, but shit with Harper had been different. She was the change that he needed in his life and now that he had experienced a change with her, the thought of it wasn't so bad. He was gonna live a little; after all, nobody wanted to be alone.

20

MISCHIEVOUS

"A boy without mischief is like a bowling ball without a liquid center."

— HOMER

"*A*unt B, when is my mommy coming to pick me up?" CJ asked as he bounced a ball, walking around the house. Bonnie had convinced Biz to allow him to walk around freely and not feel like a prisoner. CJ was oblivious to the fact that he was a hostage and Bonnie wanted to keep it that way. The last he knew, Bonnie was a friendly face, his auntie to be exact.

"Tomorrow night we'll bring you to your mom. She's excited to see you." Biz didn't say a word, just eyed the little boy. He didn't trust him, although he was only six. When Biz was six, he was mischievous and always knew what was going on around him. He didn't believe that CJ was oblivious to what this situation was. He had his guard up so high that not even a six-year-old boy could manipulate his mind. He was giving Bonnie a chance of trust and that chance was for her and only her. Although he had let Bonnie convince him to let CJ walk around the house, he watched him like an owl. It was sad to say, but he had to live on his toes. He couldn't get comfortable like he had done. Getting comfortable had almost gotten him killed. The most comfortable he had been was when he and Bonnie were alone in the house. But now with this miniature intruder, he was back to the Biz that everybody else had to see. "Are you hungry CJ?" Bonnie asked while tidying up the small mess that he had made around the house.

He shrugged his shoulders then replied. "Yes, I think I am. Can you make me something other than a sandwich?" he insisted, and Bonnie raised her brows at him. She had known CJ to be a picky eater and she knew he loved him a sandwich. The thought of him wanting her to make something else had surprised her.

"What would you like to eat?"

"Umm, spaghetti and meatballs," he replied while looking up into the sky as if he was thinking about it, while still bouncing the ball.

"I got you." She strutted to the kitchen with Biz's eyes on her. She put an extra switch in her walk because she knew he was staring, and the thought of teasing him made her smile. He knew exactly what she was doing, and he got up out his seat following her. As soon as he stepped into the kitchen, he wrapped his hands around her waist and pressed his manhood on her ass, showing her exactly what she had done.

Bonnie bit her lip and cracked a small smile while turning to face him. "Can I help you?" She loved playing the cat and mouse games with him. He lifted her by the waist and sat her on the counter swiftly, as if she weighed 10 pounds, and put his lips to hers. Bonnie put her hands to the back of his head, running her hands through his well-maintained dreads. She used her feet to try and take his sweats off, but it was almost as if something had come over him when he pulled away and listened out for the bouncing of the ball. He rushed out the kitchen and just as he had thought, CJ was up to no good.

"Hi Mommy, I wanna come home," was all he got out before Biz snatched the phone out his hand while pushing him back and knocking him over. He had known that the little boy wasn't as naïve as Bonnie thought he was. "Owwwwwe," CJ cried, and Bonnie came rushing out the kitchen. She took in the scene and already knew what CJ had done, the way that Biz was snatching the cords out the telephone to disconnect.

Bonnie shook her head, slightly upset with CJ as she helped him up to his feet. She could tell that Biz was at a hundred at the moment and decided to not say a word and just take CJ out his sight. "Make that lil' nigga a peanut butter and jelly and send his ass to the room," Biz said as Bonnie walked away, and she couldn't have agreed with him more at this point. CJ could have possibly blown her cover and she wanted to know if he had. She pulled him into the room without saying a word to him. She locked him inside and rushed back downstairs into the living room where Biz was seated with the phone on the table in front of him.

"Can they track the call?" she asked, taking a seat on the arm of the couch. He shook his head from side to side.

"My phone is programmed as an unknown number, and if it wasn't for him stopping bouncing that ball, shit could've gotten ugly," Biz replied, still visibly upset. Bonnie let out a small, deep breath and stood from where she was seated and stood behind him massaging his shoulders.

"Tomorrow, he'll be out of our hairs."

Biz closed his eyes putting his head back as the massage she gave him began to help the intensity in his shoulders. She leaned forward and kissed him on the back of his neck and ran her tongue up the side of his face and on his ear. "After tomorrow, it'll be just you, me, and this baby," she said while kissing him on his cheek and entering the kitchen to make CJ's peanut butter and jelly sandwich.

21

GROWN MAN BUSINESS

"Never spend your money before you have earned it."

— THOMAS JEFFERSON

"Ivory, count it up," Havoc instructed as he passed Ivory two duffle bags of money. Tonight was the night to get CJ, and Havoc wanted nothing more than to get him back in one piece and put bullet holes in everybody once he was out the way and safe. He had taken this money out of his own pockets. Although Harper had insisted on paying what she could, Havoc dismissed her.

In a matter of four days, their relationship had changed drastically. After being in her guts on a daily he had come to terms with the fact that once they got CJ back, they would build elsewhere. He had made his mark in Georgia and he was ready to expand and test the horizons. He wanted to make Dead Silence bigger than Georgia. He wanted to take over the entire south and that would only come with networking. He had trained Ivory up to be his protégé and he knew with the help of Ivory and his loyalty to him, Dead Silence was going to be known worldwide. Although it had only been the two of them, business was booming and having to split between just the two of them, Ivory had dollar signs for eyes. Havoc looked at Ivory and his focus and determination reminded him of himself when he was a youngin'. If he didn't know any better, he would've thought that Ivory was kin to him. Their bond came effortlessly. The bond that Havoc shared with Ivory was a different bond from anyone he had encountered. Ivory swore by Havoc; it was as if he was his god. He didn't know that Havoc saw himself in him and that he had committed enough sin in the world, and that mentoring Ivory was the one thing he knew how to do right.

Ivory opened up the duffle bag and although he had a hundred million dollars to count by hand, he didn't mind. Had it been anyone else asking him he would've declined and told them kiss his ass, but it was Havoc. Havoc could have asked him to do anything and he would have done it. He propped himself on the floor and began counting just as fast as a money machine.

"Damn Hav, you gon' really give up all this bread?" he asked curiously. Havoc had yet to ask him to come with him for the exchange and Ivory wanted to know what exactly the plan was.

Havoc shook his head. "See once I get CJ back, the money goes to the boss of the whole operation. And this bag has a tracking device embedded in it. Once the bag is in a set location, I'm making it rain on motherfuckers and getting my bread back," he explained. Ivory sat with a wide smile on his face; shit like this excited him. It was almost like playing a real life *Call of Duty* game, especially when there were guns involved.

"You one crazy nigga."

Havoc rose out his seat and went into his bedroom, and a sleeping Harper on his bed brought him some kind of solace. The feeling was foreign to him. The last woman he had been intimate with enough to have them laying in his bed, he had killed months ago. He took a seat on the bed and just thought of the predicament he was in. He knew that Harper wanted to be down for him and the thought of her being his down chick sounded good and all, but he was unsure of if he could keep her as safe as he wished to. He had already dragged her and CJ into some shit, and that alone made him question if what he was doing with her was right. He was going to be going from only worrying and caring for himself to worrying and caring for two others. The transition was too much too fast, but he wasn't gonna be the one to back down; he never did, and he wasn't going to start now.

"What you are you thinking about?" Harper asked, knowing the answer to her question. She had spent days and nights thinking about CJ and just couldn't wait to get him back. After hearing his voice on the phone, her heart cried out for him being that it was for such a short period of time. The thought of how scared he was and how much he missed her tore her to shreds, but she tried pushing the thought out her mind. She had known that the minute the phone disconnected there would be no way to trace him, and sure enough, after telling Havoc what had happened, he had made a few phone calls, and nothing. It was almost as if CJ had never even called.

"Same thing you thinking about," he replied.

"You got the money?"

"It's downstairs. Ivory is counting to make sure everything is every-thing. Now all I'm waiting on is the exchange address," he explained to her. Harper wrapped her hands around his stomach while laying her head on his back. She was comfortable with him in that way now. Havoc had been her knight in shining armor on many occasions and it only made her attraction to him grow. He had been there for her and never turned his back on her, and she was forever grateful for him and just wanted to continue to live her life with him. No man that didn't care would drop a hundred million on a kid that wasn't his. To her, that right there was love and any man that loved her child, she could love forever. CJ was fond of Havoc and the two seemed to have a connection, and Harper loved every bit of it.

"I'm coming," she said for the first time, and it was no surprise to Havoc; he had anticipated this. Of course, she wanted to be there for her child, and pushing her out would have been selfish. He wasn't going to stand in the way of that. Her coming was the exact reason why he had rethought his plan to the tracking device. He wanted to have all the smoke in the world right there at the exchange, but the risk was too much. As long as Harper and CJ weren't around, he would handle his business. He had also seen how stressed out Harper had been without her son and knew that she just needed that peace of mind that she would get the minute she saw him and knew he was okay. He nodded his head and rose up from the bed checking the clock. It was 6 p.m. and the text for the exchange location still hadn't been sent. Just as he was stepping into the bathroom, the text came through to his phone causing him to pull it out his jeans.

Unknown Number: **3764 Peachtree Boulevard 7pm**

Havoc turned on his feet seeing that the address was just about a thirty-minute drive. "Get dressed," he said to Harper as he walked out the room and back to the living room to check on Ivory. "What's the word?"

Ivory looked up at Havoc in confusion. "You did give me a hundred mil to count right? You only left for about 10 minutes. I ain't get far."

"Fuck it, we don't have time. Throw all that shit back in the bag," he instructed, and Ivory did exactly as he was told, slightly relieved that he didn't have to count anymore.

After about five minutes, Harper was walking into the living room with her hair pulled into a Chinese bun, a black, turtle neck sweater, jeans and a pair of boots. Being that Havoc had been intimate with her, his outlook on her had now changed. Everything about her screamed beauty, and he no longer saw her as Bonnie's friend. She was now his woman and he was taking that spot in her life to protect her, and tonight was going to be the ultimate test.

"I'll wait in the car," she said walking out the house, and Havoc grabbed up both duffle bags toting them on his shoulders with Ivory on his tail.

"Nah youngin', you stay right here and hold shit down. You gon' pop out with me to get my bread back, but right now, kick ya feet up and relax. This ain't that type of party. They want the bread, they gon' get it," he explained. Ivory's face went into a slight frown. Although he was now a part of the organization, he was hungry, and he just wanted to show Havoc constantly that he hadn't made the wrong decision when it came to him. He wanted to tell Havoc to let him come along and be his second pair of eyes, but he didn't want to come off as being disobedient. He knew that Havoc had his mind made up and he couldn't do anything else except fall back in line and wait to be called upon.

He watched as Havoc walked out, closing the doors behind him. Havoc was everything he wanted to be in the future, and he wasn't going to stop until he was right in his footsteps.

2 2

TWO TRUTHS AND A LIE

"A lie can travel halfway around the world while the truth is putting on its shoes."

— CHARLES SPURGEON

*B*onnie sat in the car of the parking garage that the exchange was happening in. The windows were tinted so dark that you couldn't see who was inside nor the amount of people inside. The movement of her baby was the only thing that seemed to settle her nerves. She hadn't seen her brother in months, and she wasn't sure what would be his reaction after seeing her protruding belly, but most importantly, seeing that she was with Biz. Seeing that she had chosen Biz over him, she wasn't sure how this would go because she had her own bone to pick. Harper had been hiding out the biggest secret of them all, and the actual truth of it all still shocked Bonnie.

She had believed that Harper was this innocent doctor that was just entertained about her life. She didn't know if Harper had been lying this entire time about it all or if she was the one who had fed Harper the information on how to get Khalil killed. *Why did Harper want Khalil dead?* was the question that lingered in her mind every single day since she'd found out. Khalil's death had come around full circle, but she couldn't understand the connection between the two and that was the biggest puzzle piece of them all. So yea, she was a little worried about how her twin brother would react after finding out that she had switched sides, but that was the absolute least of her worries. Besides, Havoc's biggest beef was finding out who had killed Khalil, and she had figured it out.

The only thing on Biz's mind was blowing off Havoc's head and getting his bread. He had taken long enough to recover with the damage that Havoc had done to him, and now he was ready to take his seat back at the top and if Bonnie played her cards right, she would be his first lady. He put his hand on Bonnie's thigh for reassurance. He knew what he was asking from her was no walk in the park, but it was now or never. They watched as Havoc's car pulled into the garage facing theirs. Once the car came to a stop, Bonnie reached for the door handle to get out and Biz put his hand on hers stopping her. "Patience ma, we got something that they want, so let them come out first," he schooled. Bonnie nodded her head and stared out the windshield, waiting for Havoc and Harper to come out. She could see her brother's poker face, and with the way he sat staring straight ahead, it felt like he could see her, although he couldn't. His stare was just that intense; it made her uncomfortable. After sitting for about five minutes, Biz started up the car. He knew that Havoc thought he was running this show but in reality, he wasn't.

The sound of the engine starting up caused Harper to begin slightly panicking. "They are going to leave with him if we don't get out," she said to Havoc, and he knew she was right. He opened up his door and stepped out, going straight for the backdoor grabbing both duffle bags of money. He walked directly in front of his car and sat them on the floor in front of him. That was enough for Biz to step out of his own vehicle. The sight of Biz startled Havoc, but his facial expression didn't change not even a bit. He had shot this man in the face and that alone should've killed him, but it didn't. Biz was alive and well, breathing, speaking, and still ordering motherfuckers around like he'd always done.

"Surprise motherfucker," Biz spoke sarcastically with his hands up, walking to the front of his own car as if he was walking a runway. Havoc wanted to put bullets in him right that second, but he knew that wouldn't be smart. CJ's life was still at risk, especially if Biz was behind this.

Although his blood was boiling, he decided to play it cool, playing the game that Biz wanted to play.

"Where's the boy?"

Biz chuckled, knowing that as hot headed as Havoc was, him taking his time was running him up a wall. He tapped the hood of the car and the back door of the car opened. Bonnie took a deep breath before letting her stilettos hit the cement ground. With CJ's hand in hers, she walked up to the hood of the car standing beside Biz. At this point, Havoc couldn't contain himself. His facial expression was full of surprise and shock. He wanted to ask Bonnie the obvious, but it was redundant. Her extended belly took him by surprise. All along he had known his sister was alive and well, but pregnant wasn't one of the things he thought she was. Her standing beside Biz answered all his questions.

He looked from her to Biz and the look of mockery on Biz's face made him want to put him in the dirt. He pulled his gun out his waistband and Biz matched his speed as he put his hand up. "I wouldn't do that if I were you," he said, pointing his gun at the back of CJ's head. Harper couldn't watch any longer. Although she was still in the car, no detail of the events unfolding went unnoticed. She jumped out the car walking towards CJ and Bonnie and pulled out her gun now pointing it at Bonnie.

"Mommy!!" CJ yelled as he tried walking forward, but Biz was two steps ahead of him with a grip on his sweatshirt. Harper stopped in her tracks, shocked at Bonnie's actions.

"Please don't hurt him," she begged as tears began to flow from her eyes. The mere thought of a gun behind CJ's head was driving her insane. They had come this far and all she wanted was her son back. The look on CJ's face was fearful as he looked at his mother. Harper just wanted to run to him and Havoc could tell that she was contemplating it. With Bonnie's gun aimed at her, he knew she wouldn't make it two steps towards him before she was dead. He grabbed her hand and rubbed the back of it with his thumb while pulling her towards him.

Now it was Bonnie's turn to be confused. She had clearly missed out on so much. She had never seen her brother be affectionate in this way to any women, and his kindness to Harper was taking her by surprise. After finding out Harper's big secret, she was unsure on what exactly her angle was. *Was she plotting on Havoc?* Bonnie thought.

"What the fuck is this?" she spat while waving her gun between the two of them.

"I could ask the same thing. You sleeping with the enemy B?" Havoc spoke up, showcasing disappointment in his voice. Bonnie shook her head from side to side

"Nah nigga, you sleeping with the enemy," she responded, staring a hole in Harper. Havoc had no idea what Bonnie was getting at and he wanted her to spit it out. Harper's grip on his hand got tighter because she knew that the minute he let her hand go, this would be the last time she felt his touch. Her truth was catching up with her and she had done so well hiding it, and now there was nowhere to hide. She had to come clean, but she wouldn't until Bonnie spoke up first. "Harper, you wanna tell your man what you did? Or would you like for me to do the honors?"

Harper's face went from white to bright red as fear and embarrassment took over her. Her silence was enough to let Bonnie know that she wasn't going to say a word. Havoc could sense the bullshit going on and he just wanted to know what the big secret was. He squeezed Harper's hand back causing her to wince, and the squeezing didn't stop until he felt a crack. "She put the hit out on Khalil," Bonnie said while pulling the hammer back to her gun.

The revelation of Harper's truth caused Havoc to let go of her hand as if he had been burned by fire from hell. He couldn't believe his ears and Harper's face said it all. He trained his gun from Biz to Harper. All along he had been sleeping with the enemy and had no clue. "Please, not in front of CJ," she begged, knowing her fate. Tears streamed down CJ's face and that alone caused him to retract his gun from her. "Why did you do it?" Bonnie asked while getting emotional. The truth had come out and she had been burned by someone that she would've never guessed. As she looked in Harper's eyes, she wanted to feel some kind of connection to the woman who had been her best friend for over a decade, but she felt nothing. Harper had taken her first love away and kept it a secret. She had cried and mourned Khalil's death to the same woman who had ordered it. Harper knew she owed Bonnie an explanation, but she couldn't fix her mouth to gather up the correct words.

Bonnie removed her gun from Harper's direction to behind CJ's head as well. She was going to get her to talk one way or another. "CJ is his son," she cried. There was no turning back. Havoc and Bonnie both stared at Harper with shocked faces then looked at CJ. Havoc knew she was telling the truth, meanwhile, Bonnie still couldn't believe it. Havoc had felt a connection to CJ and couldn't pin point what it was, and in reality, it was because he was his best friend's son. He had felt Khalil through him. Bonnie stared at CJ's face until she saw Khalil's, and the truth hit her hard. Khalil had betrayed her, and so had Harper. They were both in on a secret that she was oblivious to. All kinds of questions ran through her mind. *How did this happen? When did he have time to see another woman? How did I not see it?* she asked herself in her mind. She withdrew the gun from CJ's head while Biz's stayed trained on him. She put her hand onto his, pushing his hand down.

"Let him go."

Biz aimed his gun down while nodding to Havoc. "The money."

Havoc's mind was in an entirely different place. Too much had gone down in such little time and in a room full of trained killers, this wasn't a fight that anyone would win. A bullet had no name and with CJ in the room, it wasn't a risk that he was willing to take. The thought of Harper's deceit made him want to turn back around with his money, but he knew he couldn't. This was his brother's son, and he couldn't just let Biz have his way with him. Havoc grabbed both bags and walked a few steps towards Biz as Biz grabbed CJ's sweater and met him halfway. Havoc dropped the bags at his feet while grilling him. Biz nudged CJ forward, grabbing both bags with his eyes still trained on Havoc's.

"This ain't over," Havoc spat, causing Biz to chuckle.

"Oh, we is just getting started baby boy," he said, turning around and walking back towards Bonnie. Havoc wanted to take that opportunity to shoot him and Biz knew it but with Bonnie by his side, Havoc knew just as well as Biz that she was going out guns blazing as well. CJ squeezing his leg was what brought him back to reality as he picked him up and walked over to Harper with him. Harper hugged CJ as if he would disappear right before her eyes again. Bonnie and Biz jumped back in their car before slowly driving by. Harper's revelation played continuously in her mind. At first, she had been experiencing shock, secondly, she felt sadness and just as quick as those two emotions came, now she was feeling anger and betrayal. As they drove by, Bonnie rolled down the window aiming her gun out the window. There was no way that she could just leave the situation as it was. She had to act and act fast. The sound of the tires screeching caused Harper to turn around, just in time to receive her fate.

BANG! BANG! BANG!

She released three shots into Harper's chest and rolled up her window as Biz continued driving away. Harper's body went limp instantly, falling onto Havoc. CJ's screams from inside the car could be heard and all Havoc could do was hold her. He knew that Bonnie was only doing what they vowed to do. He felt bad for Harper, but he couldn't help her. Bonnie's aim was sharp as a knife, and she had done exactly what she wanted to do. He sat on the floor with Harper and watched as her life slipped away.

THE BETRAYAL

"The truth will set you free."

— JOHN 8:32

"*So much for a girls' night out!" Harper yelled over the music in the club that was blasting loudly. She and Bonnie hadn't seen each other in months and were due for a girls' night out, but of course Bonnie was all about the Benjamins and would handle work while she was having fun. To her, work was fun. She loved her work and if she could party and work, why not? Harper had been partying hard and Bonnie's eyes hadn't left her targets. She had lost count of how many drinks Harper had after the fifth one. Her homegirl was living it up for the both of them. Although it was a girls' night out, Bonnie was still on a job. She looked across the club at Khalil and he gave her a wink. With both of their eyes trained on their subject, Bonnie couldn't help but to think, this is too easy.*

Their subject was a male stripper, Valentino. He was the most popular act out and although he put on the best show for the ladies, he wasn't leaving the club with any of them. They weren't his cup of tea, but the senator was. Senator Dave McPearson, in fact, was the highlight of his life. He made Valentino come to work and feel on top of the world. Made Valentino feel like he was the only man in the world, which may have been true. Although Senator McPearson was just as fond of Valentino as Valentino was of him, Valentino couldn't tell because every time there was some kind of event the senator was stepping out with his wife. After long nights and talks with Valentino about leaving his wife for him, Valentino realized that was just a lullaby to keep him from spilling tea to the blogs. He was no dummy and he was tired of being a dummy to the senator. So after giving McPearson an ultimatum, McPearson had chosen his wife and Valentino had threatened to scream from the mountaintops about their affair. That was now where Bonnie and Khalil came in. After a ten-million-dollar wire transfer to Dead Silence, Biz had put his two best operatives up for the task.

Bonnie watched as Valentino worked the pole, while bumping and grinding on the ladies getting them all excited as bills covered his body. There was no way that one could possibly just look and know that he was gay, but Bonnie figured that was for him to know and them to figure it out. Harper stumbled beside her while getting a good glimpse at Valentino. "Man, that is some rich chocolate," she complimented. Bonnie nodded her head while slightly chuckling. She knew a secret about him that Harper didn't. Just as she was about to speak back, all the drinks that Harper had drank for the night came rushing out her mouth and onto Bonnie's heels. "Oh my, I'm sorry girl. It's about time I call it a night," she apologized while grabbing tissue off the table that was beside them.

"Damn Harp! Control ya fucking liquor," Bonnie scolded while snatching the tissue from her hand. She waved Khalil over and he could sense her energy. He had witnessed the entire thing and knew that Bonnie was in no mood to deal with her friend any longer at this point.

He strutted across the club before walking up on Bonnie and helping her clean herself up. "Can you please do me a solid and take el drunky to the house babe?"

He raised his eyebrow at her, and before he could speak up, Bonnie continued. "He's not gonna take a private dance with another man, not out here in the public. Men aren't the ones bringing money in for him, women are. It'll be easier for me than for you. I won't be long I promise.

But right now, I can't deal with this shit," she said pointing at Harper who was nodding off at the head, damn near sleep.

"You owe a nigga, B," he responded while kissing her on her cheek and walking over to Harper. He helped her up but that wasn't of much help. He swooped her off her feet cradling her like a baby as she laid her head on him. Bonnie just shook her head. She knew her best friend was fucked up and would regret it all in the morning. She had come here with the goal of getting twisted, mixing dark and light liquor, and now she was gonna feel it. She watched as Khalil walked to the bar taking a shot of 1942 before walking out the door, and she laughed to herself. There was nothing he hated more than a bitch that couldn't control her liquor. She knew that him taking that shot was what would help him deal with a drunk Harper.

* * *

"Ooh we should hit up a bar," Harper tried persuading Khalil as he drove towards the house he and Bonnie shared.

"Only place you hitting up is a bed."

Harper began to pout her face and in an instant, the song on the radio made her mood do a complete 360.

"I've been drinking, I've been drinking. I get filthy when that liquor get into me. I've been thinking, I've been thinking. Why can't I keep my fingers off you, baby? I want you, na na," she sang as she began dancing in her seat. Khalil took a glimpse of her out his peripheral vision and Harper caught right on, taking a chance to put her hands on his lap. "I want you, na na," she sang while rubbing on him.

Khalil trained his eyes on the road just as he pulled up to the house. Turning off the engine, he let Beyoncé play as Harper climbed out her seat and onto him, straddling his lap while dancing. The shot he had taken at the bar had finally settled in and with the sexual tension in the car, they both knew what they were about to do. Knowing that they were wrong was in the front of their minds but the liquor that they had consumed made them want to do something promiscuous that they would regret in the morning. A secret between the two of them that no one needed to know about.

Without a word, Harper slid her dress up and Khalil pulled his pants down. With no rubber around, the two of them knew that this was the dumbest decision they could've made yet, but the risk game them both a rush. Harper slid down slowly on his pipe and began grinding as his dick filled her up. The thought of her husband came and went as she bounced up and down on the first black man that she had shared her body with. He grabbed onto her hips, feeling the tension rise in him. He knew he was close to his climax, and so was she. The minute she clamped down on him releasing her juices all over him, he launched his missile of kids inside of her.

Harper laid her head on him while panting, closing her eyes, and he attempted to do the same. But the minute his eyes closed the only thing he could see was his woman, Bonnie. The guilt instantly ate at him and he nudged Harper off him causing her to jump up. Embarrassment filled her and she was at a loss for words just as he was. There were no words to be spoken. The same thoughts ran through both of their minds as they got themselves together and got out the car.

"Please don't tell—"

"I won't," Khalil said cutting her off, already knowing what she was going to ask of him. Fact of the matter was, Khalil had more to lose in the situation than Harper. He knew that once Bonnie found out, any hopes of them moving on with a marriage was going out the window. He knew there was nothing he could say to her that would make her want to be with him after this. He wasn't going to lose his woman because of one simple mistake. He had vowed to himself that day that this was a secret he'd take to the grave, and that was just what he did.

HARPER BEGAN SLIPPING in and out of unconsciousness, as her life began flashing before her eyes. Memories of the night CJ was conceived flashed, and it was those memories that had her exactly where she was right this minute on the floor, bleeding out in front of her son. The little bit of time that she got to spend with CJ evaded her mind. She was in so much pain and knew there was no point in fighting it. Her biggest secret had come back to bite her in the ass. In fact, it did more than bite her in the ass. It had caused her life to be taken away from her. Tears began to slip from her eyes as her vision began getting cloudy. She could hear CJ screaming at the top of his lungs and the only thing she wanted to do was console him. She had wanted nothing but the best for him and she couldn't give him that.

She and Khalil had committed the ultimate sin and paid the price, bringing an innocent child into the world and leaving him all alone with no parents. The day he had been conceived had been a mistake, but he was her greatest mistake. For him she had taken lives, something that she never would've thought she was capable of doing. And at this moment, it had hit her that she would have to face the lives of the ones she'd took. Khalil, Chris, the patients that never left her operating table. She had played god to many and now Bonnie had played god to her. She wasn't upset; in fact, she was at peace. The truth had finally gotten out. It was as if a huge weight had been taken off her shoulders. The truth that had taken so much of her to be kept a secret was out and she didn't have to hide it anymore. The only thing she regretted out of this was CJ. She loved her son with every fiber in her body, but he didn't deserve any of this. If she had known that this was the outcome of having him, then she wouldn't have. Because now here she was leaving an orphan behind. She tried to muster up all the strength in her body so that she could talk.

"CJ, baby stop crying," she whispered as she felt him sobbing on her chest. His cry was so painful to hear that it made her want to cry even more. He was living a nightmare and she knew it. At six he had witnessed his mother die right before him. The sight of that alone was enough to make a grown man cry, let alone a six-year-old. She couldn't blame him for crying but she didn't want his cries to be the last thing she heard before death fully took over her. "Mama got you always baby. Stop crying for mama. Be a big boy."

He began to wipe his tears from his face, just hoping that if he listened to his mother that she would be able to live, but it didn't work that way. When it was your turn to go it was your turn, and he was realizing that with every breath that his mother took.

"I love you CJ. You are going to grow to become a strong man, and I'm going to be very proud of you. I'm always going to be with you baby.

Now Mommy got to go. But you are safe with Uncle Rara. I love you baby."

"I love you too," he mustered out. And those were the last words that Harper heard as the grim reaper took her to her maker.

Havoc knew she was gone. With his head back against the wall and Harper's head in his lap, a million thoughts ran through his head. The biggest thought of them all being that CJ was his responsibility. He took a deep breath before finally getting up off the floor and scooping Harper into his arms. He opened the back door and laid her dead body across the backseat. He let CJ sit in the passenger seat as he continued to cry. The responsibility of a kid to Havoc was so much to bear. He had raised Ivory up to be just like him and he wanted different for CJ. He knew that if Khalil was alive that he would want different for his son, and Havoc just wasn't 100% sure that he was capable of giving him that.

ABOUT THE AUTHOR

My name is Diaka Kaba and I am from the Bronx, NY. I have always had a passion for reading since the third grade. At the time Barbara Parks Junie B. Jones series were godly to me. As I got older picking up The Coldest Winter Ever by Sister Soulja is what got me hooked to Urban fiction. I began writing on Wattpad for fun and I got signed to my first publishing company Shan Presents. When I became a teen mom I put the pen down for a while then realized that every job I worked made me miserable and that writing was my true passion and what made me happy. The author who inspires me the most is Ashley Antoinette. My dream is to one day become New York's Best Selling Author.

Stay Connected:
Email me questions at DIAKASKABA@GMAIL.COM
I will be answering questions about Honesty and Ahmad on my YouTube channel, DAK's Corner.

Royalty Publishing House is now accepting manuscripts from aspiring or experienced urban romance authors!

WHAT MAY PLACE YOU ABOVE THE REST:

Heroes who are the ultimate book bae: strong-willed, maybe a little rough around the edges but willing to risk it all for the woman he loves.

Heroines who are the ultimate match: the girl next door type, not perfect - has her faults but is still a decent person. One who is willing to risk it all for the man she loves.

The rest is up to you! Just be creative, think out of the box, keep it sexy and intriguing!

If you'd like to join the Royal family, send us the first 15K words (60 pages) of your completed manuscript to submissions@royaltypublishing-house.com

LIKE OUR PAGE!

Be sure to <u>LIKE</u> our Royalty Publishing House page on Facebook!

CPSIA information can be obtained
at www.ICGtesting.com
Printed in the USA
LVHW052143070519
616961LV00003B/421

9 781095 754245